With his last valiant effort, the broom handle once again skated over the worm...and flew from his hands.

Shit...oh shit...oh fuck...

The lips peeled back, the teeth slid out and Geno felt piss run down his leg as the worm darted at him, teeth slashing. He ducked out of its way once, then twice...then he tried to seize it in his hands, but it was like trying to take hold of a canned ham thick with aspic jelly...his fingers just slid over its bloated, slimed segments, its bristles cutting into the palms of his hands.

He thought it would bite him, tear his face off, but it didn't. The mouth closed and the bulblike head snapped forward like a fist, striking him in the chest and flattening him. The wind knocked out of him, he hit the floor, dazed and confused. It felt like his sternum had been split open like a dry sheaf of corn.

When he opened his eyes, the mouth was inches from his face.

The teeth were gleaming like scalpels

WORM

by TIM CURRAN

1

L ike most days, it began badly.

Before Charise left for work, she told Tony to remember to walk Stevie. To take him out for a brisk run through the park to get his heart going and his blood pumping because it was good for his health and longevity. Not Tony's, of course—hell, he was just her husband—but the dog. *Stevie.* Which was a perfectly gay sort of name for a dog as far as Tony was concerned, but then again Stevie was a perfectly gay sort of dog: half-Pomeranian and half-Poodle. Something dog-loving Charise called a lap-dog and something Tony himself called simply embarrassing.

Lap-dog? No, it's a boot-dog. In that when it starts yipping in its gay little voice, you give it a kick.

Charise did not find that funny at all. She also didn't find it amusing when he asked her to get rid of the ugly little carpet-crawler and get a real dog: a Lab or a Collie or a Shepherd.

No, she scooped the little mutt up and kissed its homely pushed-in face. "But mama loves her little puppy, her little baby, her little Stevie-weevie." Kiss, kiss, smooch-smooch. Jesus. It was enough to make you fucking sick.

When Tony finally got his ass out of bed from his afternoon nap, stretched and yawned, the little beggar was waiting for him. And, oh boy, the look in his eyes. It was almost as if Stevie understood exactly how things worked. That Mama Charise tugged the purse strings and Tony was an unemployed slob, a second-class citizen, a subservient domestic that washed the floor and answered the phone, scrubbed the toilet and made casseroles and walked little Stevie-weevie and cleaned up his accidents on the living room carpet. That Mama Charise wore his balls on a choker chain around her throat, and when she said jump, Tony asked not only how high but if he should do a fucking backflip and a double pirouette while he was up there.

God, it was like the damn dog understood.

"Okay, mutt," Tony said. "Let me work the kricks out of my back and take a leak and then we'll go."

Stevie barked…well, it was more of a little yip. If Gollum were a dog, he'd bark like that.

Stevie stared at him. *Okay, you lazy slob, but make it quick because I ain't getting any younger here and my bladder ain't what it once was, capiche?*

"Fuck you," Tony said, aiming a kick at the mutt.

Stevie dodged and bared his teeth. Then he made with the staring eyes again. *You wanna watch it, you useless slug. I tell Mama about this and Mama will throw your dead ass out into the street. You don't wanna make her choose between us. You don't want that at all.*

The phone rang. Sighing, Tony grabbed up the cordless. "Yeah?" he said.

"Hey, Tony." Stephani from next door, she of the perfect body and blonde hair, the liquid green eyes that made his knees feel weak. "This is Steph. Charise told me to call you. Remind you to walk the dog."

"How considerate of her."

"Oooh, you sound cranky. Well, don't shoot the messenger."

"Sorry."

"So what's on your busy schedule today besides walking Stevie?"

The sarcasm, the sarcasm. "I'm wide open today. Tonight, I got a date with a pool cue."

"Ooooo," she said. "I'd like a date with a pool cue."

"Like it would be the first time."

"Ha. Well, I just got out of the shower and I can't stand here naked, dripping all over everything, now can I?"

Shameless little flirt. "I could bring over a towel," he said, imagining it, picturing it in all its pornographic glory.

"You wish. No, not this time. I'll rub myself dry."

"You had your chance."

She laughed.

Click.

Ah, yes. Little Miss Perfect Stephani Kutak. She knew he wanted her as all men wanted her and it amused her. She was a little tease. Yet, for all of that, her little flirty phone calls were about the only bright spot in his somewhat dull existence. At least they broke up the monotony.

Tony stumbled off into the bathroom, noticing that Charise had left a list of chores for him to do and errands to run. It wasn't like the old days. No little heart drawn at the bottom of the list or *Love ya, honey. Char!* No, she knew his place and treated him as such. *Just get it done, will ya?* Tony sighed and made his way to the head. Christ, she left her curling iron out again, cans of hairspray and gel and facial goo, a dozen long, dark hairs in the sink he scrubbed out yesterday. It looked like something hairy was trying to claw its way up out of the drain.

Sighing again, he freed his manhood, which didn't look particularly manly today...kind of like a snail that was afraid to come out of its shell. He directed his stream, wondering what to make Her Highness for supper tonight. Stevie yipped impatiently again and Tony scowled.

Then the house began to tremble.

What the hell is that?

Pissing was suddenly of little interest. The house shook enough to rattle the mirror over the sink. Right away, he thought maybe it was a big truck passing by—a very *big* truck—but that didn't explain it. No, as absurd as it sounded, it was as if a fist gripped the house and shook it like a snow globe.

When it happened again, he knew it wasn't coming from outside.

It was coming from far below where the bad things grow.

2
_____

Three doors down, Tessa Saldane gripped the arms of her recliner as a low-level rumbling shook everything up, knocking knickknacks off shelves and pictures off hooks. The windows rattled. A Currier & Ives print thudded to the hardwood floor of the dining room, its glass face shattering.

This more than anything got her out of the recliner. She originally thought it was one of those damn jets again, coming in low on its approach to the Price County airport. Now and again, whether by design or accident, they liked to swoop down and set things to rattling as they passed over the rooftops of Pine Street and Twenty-first Avenue.

But this was no jet.

In fact, Tessa didn't know what in the hell it was.

When she got to her feet—and sometimes when she was settled in like that, it took some doing—it felt like the house was…well, *wobbling*. Like it wasn't sitting on solid terra firma but something loose and rolling like Jell-O. As Tessa stood there, not daring to move, everything seemed to be in motion and she was sure she would be spilled to the floor violently. And when you're on the wrong side of seventy like Tessa, an impact of that sort had a way of dislocating your knees and breaking your hips, neither of which would knit up quite the same again…if at all.

So she stood there, feeling a disturbing fright down low in her belly that pushed cold, reaching fingers up into her chest.

The house shook again and, *dammit*, she heard her mother's Haviland eggshell tea set hit the kitchen floor and break into pieces.

Lord, what now? Whatever now?

Of course, she was thinking *earthquake*…but whoever heard of an earthquake in Camberly, which sat smack-dab in the middle of solid green-grassed, blue-skied, hay-mowed Price County? This was the Midwest for godsake. Things like that might happen out in California and god-awful places like that—and Tessa wouldn't have been the one to say they didn't have it coming with the way they carried on out there—but not here.

Now the rumbling, which sounded oddly like a very hungry belly, had ceased and was replaced by a *glub-glub-glub* sort of noise. It reminded her of wet cement poured into a well-tamped sidewalk frame. Only it sounded not so much like it was poured, but gurgling up from a drain.

By the time Tessa made her way to the picture window that looked out on green, serene Pine Street, the vilest sort of sewer smell filled the house. It definitely stank of drains, the backed-up kind. It was a rank odor of decay, subterranean drainage, and hot rotten egg sulfur. *Gah.*

At the window, she felt herself deflate.

So much for green and serene Pine Street. There was some kind of black muck oozing up through cracks in the street, flowing up and over curbs and washing into yards. As she watched, dumbfounded, the green grass was drowned in a sluicing black, fetid flow and a great mound began to rise from Bertie Kalishek's front yard across the street. It was like a great bubble expanding beneath the grass. It had to be twelve or fifteen feet across.

It kept rising like a cake, the sod splitting open above it like the flesh of a diseased sore, black muck draining from it like pus. About the time the bubble, or whatever it was, had the circumference of a child's wading pool and stood tall as a man...it burst. Like a boil, it popped open, exploding with a spray of black goo that spattered the exterior of the Kalishek house.

It looked like a giant had thrown a handful of loose, runny shit right at the neat white clapboarding.

The black muck that built up under the bubble flowed through the yard, slopping up against the porch steps. Like an open wound, it continued to bleed in copious quantities until the Kalisheks' yard was...gone, drowned under a good two or three feet of gushing black foulness.

Tessa didn't know what it was.

She thought at first it was oil.

But this wasn't Oklahoma and this stuff was too thick, too congested, too much like plain old mud from a river bottom... smelled like it, too, only worse. It occurred to her—and not without some humor—that it looked much like diarrhea, black and sloshing and even foul (though *foul* isn't the word she thought originally, but *unclean*).

God only knew what diseases and contaminates the stuff might carry.

The very idea made her shudder.

As Tessa continued to watch, the spit drying up in her mouth, she noticed more bubbles rising. Immense things that expanded with a rubbery, tearing sort of sound as they split open lawns. One of them—at the Desjardins' down the block—rose up an easy ten or fifteen feet and another—at the Jungs'—was twice that size, like an immense cancerous blister on the good old earth. It lifted up most of the Jungs' front yard, the sidewalk and driveway cracking open like sheets of ice. A rickety potting shed in the side yard tipped over and shattered.

You should call somebody, you should do something, Tessa thought as the Kalisheks' front porch was turned into scrap wood by yet another bubble. Black goo flooded through the neighborhood in a rising tide. There was another low rumble and the ground shook.

Pressure was building below.

One after the other, more bubbles popped like suppurating wounds, their blood splashing out in dark, fluid tangles. There was a thudding, creaking noise and a manhole cover exploded into the air and hit the curb with a clanging sound, gouging out a chunk of concrete. Instead of sinking into the goo, it rolled right through the Mackenridges' front yard, splitting Kathleen's wishing well right in two before smashing into the porch. Though the mouth of the manhole itself was underneath the black, boggy river now, its location was marked by a constant *glub-glub-glub* as more of that filth bubbled out, gushing and rippling.

Two doors down, Tessa saw Mr. Green waddle through the slop to his car and jump in. He backed out into the street and became instantly mired. He tried rocking the car back and forth; then it stalled. He jumped out, swearing and shouting, slipping beneath the muck and coming up looking like he'd been tarred.

Tessa couldn't help giggling under her breath at that.

Glub-glub-glub.

She turned. This time it was coming from *inside* not outside. It made her shiver…it was a very *bad* sort of sound.

A piercing scream echoed outside, somewhere down the block, and Tessa tensed with terror. The scream came again, then faded off into a lot of yelling and shouting. She tried to see through the window where it was coming from, but couldn't.

"God, what now?"

When she looked back for Mr. Green, he was nowhere to be seen. His car looked like an island out there in the fuming cesspool of mud. One door was still open. People were gathered on porches but no other fools were willing to join him for a dip in the slimy muck.

Glub-glub-glub.

Dammit. There it was again.

Tessa crossed the living room and traced the sound to the bathroom. The sink was half-full with bubbling black sludge. The toilet water looked like ink. And again, using bathroom analogies, she decided it looked like the mother of all messy dumps.

Glub-glub-glub.

From the kitchen!

Pained and distressed, Tessa arrived to see glops of chunky black ooze dropping from the faucet into her shiny, clean stainless steel sink. *Plop, plop, plop.* More of it dropped, looking almost like it was ejected from pressure.

Oh, not my new sink, not my new sink.

She instinctively grabbed the spigot, hoping to wash that filth down into the drain. No water came out, just more of the glistening ebon slush.

And this was all bad enough with the mess and the stink that reamed out her nose, but in the three or so inches of slop, she saw movement.

Not bubbling.

Something else.

A weird, almost serpentine shape.

There was something alive in the sink.

3

Sitting on his porch, Geno Desjardins watched the muck flowing in sluicing, gelid channels through the neighborhood. It was already lapping up to the third stair on the porch. The mess and the smell were bad enough, but the cleanup would be very expensive, astronomical even. It would drive everyone's insurance rates right through the roof and the time it would take...not good.

He'd just gotten off his cell with his brother on the other side of Camberly and the muck was in the streets over there, too, filling them like a cup.

What a fucked-up mess.

Ivy came out and handed Geno a beer that he nearly emptied on the first swallow. She sat down, nervously puffing on a cigarette. It looked like a long, sleek white missile, afterburners blazing as she pulled on it.

"It's getting worse," she said.

"Yes, it is."

"Should we try and drive out of it?"

"In *that?*"

Exasperated, scared, smoke fuming from her nostrils like foundry stacks, she said, "Well, anything would be better than drowning in it...don't you think?"

"It won't rise much more."

"Says you."

Geno ignored her. It was a hobby of his. He'd already been on the phone with Public Works and they were responding to similar incidents all over town. The mayor had contacted the governor and the National Guard was being mobilized to set up temporary structures outside of town for those forced from their homes. The Army Corps of Engineers was on its way.

All of which was great, Geno figured. He was glad to see his tax dollars at work. But none of it answered one very basic question:

what in the hell was this stuff? It wasn't sewage exactly or mud or gray water or seepage, but maybe some weird combination of all those things and a few others to boot.

Disgusting, that's what.

"We'll wait it out for the time being. If it gets too deep, we'll make a run for it."

But Ivy didn't like that in the least.

She was far too hyper and far too neurotic to sit around waiting. She paced from one end of the porch to the other, mumbling under her breath and chain-smoking. She favored Virginia Slims 120s. They were as long as No. 2 pencils. She'd smoke one halfway down, frantically puffing at it, then toss it over the railing and fire up another one. In the fifteen minutes she'd been on the porch, she'd killed three of them.

Geno knew better than to mention the fact.

"Look," she said.

He turned and peered across the street.

Mr. Green was backing out into the sludge, trying to make a break for it. His car dogged out almost instantly. Geno chuckled low under his breath as Green got out, slipped and went under, came up swearing and snorting.

"Aren't you going to help him?" Ivy wanted to know.

"Let me think about it," he said. Then: "*No.*"

Why the hell would he help Green? The guy was a prying, spying, nosey asshole who constantly called the police on his neighbors for everything from backyard bonfires to loud music to their garages not being up to code.

No, this was entertainment. He wasn't about to help that tubby sonofabitch.

Green kept slipping and sliding, covered in black mud now.

Everyone in the neighborhood was watching, but nobody was helping. The comedy was too rich, like discovering Buster Keaton for the first time.

Ivy was mad, of course. She stalked into the house and slammed the screen door. She would go back into the kitchen now, Geno knew, and reorganize the cupboards for the fifth or sixth time, making sure all the spices were arranged alphabetically.

He finished his beer, giggling at Green.

Then Ivy screamed.

4

Eva Jung sat at the kitchen table, studying her fingers on the tablecloth. They were the one thing she took great comfort from, those long, slender fingers of hers. Though the knuckles were now arthritic and swollen, the fingers themselves were still quite handsome, she thought, the nails smooth and manicured.

Though she was by all appearances a frail woman and most on Pine Street believed she wasn't exactly baking with a hot oven, Eva's mind was quite sharp. Sharp enough to know her neighbors were conspiring against her. They disliked her because her grass was often too long and her weeds unplucked, her fence falling over and the house badly in need of painting...but these things were not her fault. Leonard was no longer here and he had always taken care of such things. She hired a boy to attend to the yard work in the summer, but only once a month.

Ever since Leonard died, she came out of her big old house only rarely and mostly at night when her neighbors could not watch her.

She did not like to be watched.

Or listened to.

Or even noticed.

When the muck rose from beneath the earth and laid waste to her yard, she was really not that surprised. In the back of her mind she had been expecting catastrophe for years.

Through carefully parted Venetian blinds, she watched it flow and gurgle.

It would be dark soon. She knew what would happen then: the monsters would come....just as they came for her when she was a little girl shivering in her bed. Long-armed and red-eyed, they'd come creeping out of the darkness, slithering and hungry.

When Ivy Desjardins screamed, distracting the others, Eva kept her eyes on Mr. Green out in the road, fighting his way from his stalled car in the mud sea. She was the only one on Pine Street that saw him go under for the last time just as she was the only one that saw what grabbed him.

Monsters. There are monsters in the muck.

5

A t the Albert household, Tony was on his ass.

The house had not only shaken, it had shifted...and enough to knock him off his feet. Earthquake, it had to be a goddamn earthquake. His bladder still full and Stevie yipping like the little pansy he was, Tony got up and carefully walked over to the window. He stepped lightly as if his weight would bring the house down around him.

Holy shit.

He saw the black muck oozing in the streets, flooding and surging and slopping through yards. There was wreckage in the neighborhood. Porches damaged and picnic tables flipped over, lots of assorted junk floating in the mud sea—everything from inflatable pools to bird feeders to clumps of decorative shrubbery.

A mudslide? Is that what this is?

It was the first thing he thought. Like out in California where heavy rains washed out entire hillsides and the houses built atop them. But for something like that to happen there had to be a whole lot of rain to create enough mud for a slide in the first place, and they hadn't gotten much of that lately.

Then what? What?

Stevie yipped at his heels.

"Shut the fuck up," Tony told him.

The mud was everywhere, flowing and sluicing, seeming to rise as he watched. Where the hell was it all coming from?

The cordless rang. He saw on the caller ID that it was Marv O'Connor from down the block. "You seeing this shit, Tony?"

"Am I ever. What the hell is it about?"

"I don't know, but I think our pool game is canceled for tonight."

Tony laughed. "You're lucky. I was going to show you a few moves."

"I bet you were."

It was an inside joke: Tony had lost fourteen of the last twenty weekly games. He owed Marv over two-hundred bucks, but Marv knew he'd never get it just as Tony knew he'd never pay it. They were both okay with that.

"Well, you get bored over there, put on your waders and come over. Fern is making steak sandwiches. I'm providing the beer."

Tony grinned. Marv brewed his own beer. It was strong stuff. The last time Tony drank some—an odd coconut-flavored concoction—he got so drunk he fell off the porch and threw up on himself. Twice.

"Sounds good, but if I come, I have to bring Gollum with me."

"Ah, the kids love Stevie. Bring him over." Marv laughed. "You know, you two are closer than you think."

Tony set down the phone and, right away, his cell rang. Grand Central Station today.

If was another political call, he was going to puke. *Vote for me because I am honest and hardworking and middle-class just like you. I am not a money-grubbing prick taking money under the table and dry-fucking the people who put me into office. There is not one drop of corporate jism on my chin.*

But it wasn't another desperate politico, it was Charise calling from her office. "Tony...oh my God...do you see what's happening out there?"

"Yeah. I'm looking at it right now."

"It's going on all over town. They're saying it's coming up from below."

"How can that be?"

"That's what they're saying. You better get out of there."

He laughed dryly. "Really? And how am I supposed to do that? There's got to be three feet of black, runny shit in the streets. My little Celica would bog-down in ten feet."

"Is Stevie okay?"

Is Stevie okay? Yeah, this woman was precious, all right. She had a tipped uterus and couldn't have children, so she pressed her maternal, adoring, totally fucked-up mother love onto that hairball. It would have been funny if it wasn't so goddamn pathetic. Like some crazy, dried-up old bag lady pretending her dolls were real children or the thirty stray cats in her living room were some kind of extended family. He didn't even like to think about all the times she'd embarrassed him in public because of that damn dog. Other women (ones that weren't fucking nuts) would show pictures of their kids and Charise, true to form as the bug-job she was, whipped out pictures of that mangy little turd on her iPhone. Stevie napping. Stevie playing with his ball. Stevie with his faggoty winter sweater on. Stevie sitting on her lap (probably afraid that Donna Peppek's aged feline, Buttercup, would knock the piss out of him). Dear God. All the other women would get that look on their faces—sympathy and remorse for Char's decaying mind and barren womb, and the guys would just turn away. *Poor Tony, he married a real head case.*

"Tony? Tony? Is Stevie okay?"

No, some gerbils beat the hell out of him and then gang-fucked him. Sorry, hon. Now how's about we get a real dog? One that I don't have to feel ashamed of?

"He's fine. He's pussying up in the corner as usual."

"Tony!"

"Be nice if you asked about me sometime."

"Be serious," she said.

"I thought I was."

She sighed heavily. "Well, just sit tight. They're supposed to be evacuating people."

"Tell 'em to hurry. The only meat in the house is your fucking hamster and he's going on the barbie at five sharp."

"Tony! You can't—"

Crackle, crackle.

"Charise? Char?"

Nothing. No bars. No service. For once, he was thankful for their shitty cell carrier.

Stevie yipped and Tony threw the phone at the miserable little rat-dog. More yipping. More hopping and nails scratching over the tile floor. *Keep it up, you little fairy. Mama ain't nowhere around. You get out of line and you're going out into the muck.* Stevie seemed to understand; he quieted right away.

Well, since there was nothing to do but wait it out, Tony lit a cigarette and sighed with satisfaction. Charise didn't allow smoking in the house. Too fucking bad. What did it matter now? Goddamn place was sinking like a brick.

Glug, glug.

As he watched, some oily black ooze dripped from the faucet and splatted into the sink. Not good. Well, Charise was right then: it *was* coming up from below.

Tony took a pull on his cigarette and went over to the head to drain the vein. Maybe circumstances were dire, but there was no need to suffer with a full bladder. He pulled himself out and started to pee. There. That was better. When he finished, he flushed…and left the seat up. Most men generally forgot, he knew, and pissed off their wives. Then there were the other guys who did it on purpose because their wives were infatuated with butt-ugly dogs and—

What the fuck now?

The toilet flushed, making a weird gurgling sound like it was choking on what it had swallowed…then it barfed up something: a black, shifting mass. It was stuffed into the siphon hole at the bottom rear of the tank. Something shiny like wet rubber. His first thought was that Charise dropped a real bomb and it had come slinking its way back up, but, no, it wasn't that at all.

Hell is that?

Stevie yipped.

"Quiet," Tony grumbled.

Now, if it was your ordinary large but inoffensive turd down there, it would slowly, through suction, be drawn farther into the siphon. But the reverse was true. This…*object*…was pushing its bulk *into* the tank, not being pulled *out*. It had to be more of that crap coming through the lines. The water began to darken like India ink.

The mass at the very bottom continued to expand.

Tony's eyes widened.

That shiny mass began to look very much like a blunt snout.

He stepped back as the snout pushed its way into the bowl with a slow, oily, corkscrewing motion. It was alive. It was moving. Not being moved by the water or suction, but moving of its own accord.

Shit.

He thought of those stories about snakes getting into the plumbing. Maybe they weren't urban legends after all.

The thing…snake, worm…whatever in the hell it was, twisted itself out of the siphon. Tony tripped over his own feet and fell backward, thumping the back of his head against the tub and seeing a few stars.

Flat on his back, he heard Stevie come padding in.

Stevie looked down at him as the thing splashed around in the bowl. *What'd you do this time, fool?* the look in Stevie's eyes seemed to say, but Tony was not very interested in what Stevie was thinking because he saw the snout of the thing peeking up over the rim of the toilet like a cobra rising from a snake charmer's basket.

Stevie cocked his little head and yipped.

Tony made a gasping sound in his throat, pulled himself up on his ass and shoved Stevie back into the living room. By the time he found his feet, scrambling to them with white fear breaking loose in his chest, the thing had filled the toilet…and then the toilet exploded.

It went off like a bomb with a thundering eruption, porcelain flying in shards, water and filthy goo spraying up the walls and flooding the bathroom floor.

The thing was loose.

Tony saw it coiled among the remains of the bowl. He figured it was probably an easy three or four feet in length, stout and evil-smelling. It writhed and looped like an earthworm in the sun, dirty brown going to slate gray, its segmented body exuding a clear slime.

It had no eyes.

But it did have a mouth.

With a hissing sound, the mouth opened, seeming to shrivel back from pink jaws lined with long, needlelike teeth…many, many teeth. So many, they were like the spokes of a bike tire.

It was getting ready to strike.

With a cry, Tony tossed the clothes hamper at it just as it moved. It bought him bare seconds but no more. It was not stopped by the hamper, not in the least. In fact, it drilled right through it, corkscrewing with immense velocity and punching through the wicker in a cloud of fragments.

Tony managed to throw the door shut behind him.

But he had no time to secure the lock.

The creature hit the inside of the door with such force that it slammed shut. It hit it again and put a dent in it, the wood splintering as it split lengthwise. Then, from the other side, a sound like the claws of a dozens rats scratching manically…but Tony knew it was not claws but teeth. The thing was chewing right through the fucking door.

Stevie was yipping.

Tony was speechless.

He stood there uneasily, tense with fear and anxiety, his own voice droning in his head: *Am I seeing this? Am I really fucking seeing this? A monster from the toilet? A beast from the bowl?* But by then those teeth on the other side had eaten through, tearing a hole right through the door. The hole wasn't big enough for it to fit through, not just yet.

But it was determined.

Unbelievably, savagely determined.

Tony knew he had to keep pressure against the door or the damn thing would knock it right off its hinges, but there was no way he was pressing his back against it. He could just about imagine what that thing would do to his unprotected back if it went through the hamper that quickly and chewed a hole in the door itself.

Christ, he didn't want to think about it.

Stevie continued to yip and Tony shouted at him to shut up, which, as usual, only got him yipping that much louder and that much more shrilly.

The worm—Jesus, it had to be a worm because it sure as hell wasn't a snake—kept hitting the door with maximum thrust. The door was only a cheap panel job. Something designed to look nice, but with absolutely no tensile strength. It was cracking open. Chips of paint and wood splinters were flying in the air.

It gnawed another hole through.

Tony was glad he pissed or he would have gone right down his leg by that point.

Think! Think! Think! There's gotta be something you can do!

But he knew there really wasn't. To do something meant he'd have to quit pushing against the door and as soon as he stopped doing that, Mr. Worm was going to tear him a new asshole. Literally.

Stevie yipped louder.

The door was coming apart.

Tony was scared shitless.

Another hole appeared, this one down by his knee. He saw the bulblike snout of the worm press through. A ribbon of black slime hung from its mouth like drool.

Then it withdrew.

It stopped pounding itself against the door.

Tony listened.

He heard a distinctly appalling slithering sound, which must have been the worm sliding across the tile floor. There was a splashing, wet sort of noise and he dared to hope it had gone back down the pipe. But the thing was so furious and relentless in its attack, the idea seemed ludicrous. Things like it did not give up until they got what they were after.

It was quiet in the bathroom.

He heard water dripping, nothing else.

Even Stevie had quit yipping.

Toilet water flowed under the door and Tony was standing in a rank, chill pool of it. He waited. A minute, two, then three. Gradually, he eased off on the door. He expected the worm to batter it, but it didn't.

It was absolutely silent in there.

He looked over at Stevie and the little mutt cocked his head in that way Charise thought was so cute. But he was not trying to be cute, Tony knew. The cocked-head thing was the dog's version of *what the fuck?* That's all it was and all it had ever been, despite Charise's human need to pretend otherwise.

His heart thudding in his chest, Tony moved away from the door.

Damn, it looked like it had been hit repeatedly by hammers. *Big* fucking hammers. It was hard to believe that a single—albeit large and freaky—worm could cause that much damage. Worms were soft-bodied creatures and maybe somebody needed to remind this thing of that.

It was still silent in there.

Stevie looked up at him with the same WTF look and Tony gave it back to him. *What the fuck, indeed.* He felt a curious camaraderie with the little mutt. They'd always actively despised each other, but he felt that had somehow changed now. Common desperation and common fear had linked them together in a universe of mutual need. Wouldn't Charise be surprised—and hurt—when Stevie started hanging out with him?

Tony crouched down by the dog and ruffled his fur.

"I hope to God that thing is gone," he whispered.

"Either way, we better get the hell out of here before it gets back."

So that was the plan. But plans required action and action

meant moving and that meant turning his back on the door and he did not like the idea of that at all. But it was silent in there and he didn't honestly believe the worm could play possum quite that well.

He stood up slowly.

He wrinkled his nose at the foul stench coming from the bathroom. He couldn't put a finger on what it was exactly, some kind of weird, dank smell of shit and piss, fungal rot and maggoty decay. Horrible.

"Stand guard, Stevie. You hear anything in there, yip your head off."

He pretty much thought he was talking to himself, but as he backed away into the hallway, Stevie stayed right there, fixing the door with a steely, resolute glare. Tony jogged into the bedroom and peeled off his wet socks. He pulled off his joggers and slipped into some jeans, threw on a hoodie and put dry socks on. That was better. He got his backpack out of the closet. He'd stuff bottled water and food in there. Enough to last them until they got free of town anyway.

When he got back, Stevie was still manning...or *dogging*...his post.

Tony threw on his gum rubber snow boots and grabbed his softball bat out of the closet. Maybe it wasn't the best weapon, but it was hardwood and it could easily split skulls and, hopefully, worms.

"Okay, Stevie," he said. "I'm going to look in there. I think it's gone but I have to know for sure."

Stevie gave him one of his looks. *What? You want the worm to eat you?*

Tony went to the door and, without hesitation, opened it, a white bolt of fear digging down deep into his belly.

Nothing.

The bathroom was an absolute mess, but he saw no worm. Nothing in the tub. Nothing in the sink. The toilet had pretty much exploded, nothing left but its base, which was bolted securely to the floor, and the black, ugly outgoing pipe and its flange.

Tony sighed, releasing his death grip on the bat.

It was a fluke. That worm was some mutant that had been growing in the putrid darkness down there for years. One of a kind.

It's gone back and will probably die before anyone else ever sees it.

This was what he told himself and it made him feel better. Much better, in fact…though he knew he'd never be able to sit bare-assed on a toilet again, exposing himself to subterranean, worming horrors.

"Okay, Stevie, let's be sheep and get the flock out of here," he said. "Let's go visit Stephani or drop in on the O'Connors."

Then, from the pipe, there was a splashing sound. It was more than just water and he knew it.

"Shit," he said.

6

"What is it now?"

"Down here!" Kathleen cried. "Hurry for godsake!"

Pat Mackenridge sighed. He looked out the window at his Dodge Ram sitting in the driveway. Then he turned and went down the hallway. "Where the hell are you?"

"I'm down here! Hurry up!"

God, this better be good. This better be something real good, something applicable. If he got down there and she was panicking because a stupid fucking spider had crawled out from under the dryer, he was going to lose it. Really lose it.

"Are you coming or what?"

She sounded frantic now.

He jogged down the steps, stopping just before he reached the basement floor. "What?"

She grumbled in her throat. "Can you be bothered to come down all the way or do I have to come over there and guide you by the hand?"

Oh, that mouth.

He stepped down into the basement and smelled it right away, the same stink as outside but concentrated down here…an almost violent stench of moist rot, corruption, and sewer slime. The black gunk was foaming up out of the floor drain by the hot water heater, a slushy filth that popped with greasy-looking bubbles. To Pat, it smelled the way he imagined animal carcasses might when stranded by the receding waters of a flood.

Wrinkling his nose, he said, "Screw it. Let's just get out of here."

"Our house," Kathleen lamented. "Our…*home*."

He put an arm around her. She was stiff as a plank. It was like trying to comfort a fencepost. "We'll come back when this is over and fix everything up. The important thing is to get out of here."

"Do you think it'll really get that bad?"

"I don't know. I really don't."

"Maybe we should wait," she suggested.

"No."

"No?"

"No, Kathleen. That shit is getting deep in the streets. I think it's still rising. If we wait too long, even my truck won't go through it. I think we can clear it right now, but in another hour…I just don't know."

"I don't like the idea of getting trapped out there, Pat. It'll be dark in an hour. And with the baby…"

"We don't have a choice."

He didn't wait for any more arguments.

He mounted the stairs and as he started to climb them, Kathleen coming after him for another round of debate, there was a sound from within the cellar wall like somebody had cracked an egg. It got louder. It became a grinding, tearing sound. The seam between two concrete blocks split and black ooze bubbled out like crude oil.

"Oh shit," Kathleen said.

They rushed up the stairs.

"The ground's saturated," Pat told her, pulling on his rubber hip waders. "I read once that during floods, the water doesn't come in under the door or through the walls so much as it just seeps up through the foundation. That's what's happening now."

Kathleen started to argue again, but closed her mouth.

Abandoning her home did not come easy to her, but she knew he was right. They just couldn't wait around. Maybe if it had just been the two of them, but baby Jesse changed all that. They couldn't afford to take chances.

Pat pulled on his raincoat—he wasn't really sure why—and stepped out onto the porch.

As he moved down the steps, Kathleen grabbed his arm. "No," she said.

"What?"

"I've got a really bad feeling. Don't go out there."

He wasn't in the mood for her premonitions. Now of all goddamn times. He went down and stepped into the muck. It was oddly warm, thick and slopping like oatmeal. It seemed to have the same degree of thickness. He trudged through it over to the Dodge. He would back it up to the porch and Kathleen and the baby could get in and off they'd go. A simple plan, really.

By the time he got to the truck, the muck was up to his thighs.

The Dodge was high-profile, but even so the mud was up over the tires. Maybe it was too late. Maybe they would have to wait it out. Get upstairs and hope for the best.

No, dammit. They had to get out.

Kathleen was on the porch.

"Get Jesse ready," he said.

At the moment he said that, he felt something move against his leg. There were probably all kinds of things bobbing in the muck, but this one *moved*. It brushed against his knee, then against the side of his other leg. The muck moved with secret eddies and ripples like a moat in a fairy tale.

What the hell?

He was about to call out to Kathleen when something hit his right ankle, gripping it in a crushing embrace, twisting it. He made a grunting sound and dropped into the mud, submerging in it. It flowed into his mouth and down his throat. He fought and thrashed in unbelievable panic as he was towed away with a violent jerking underneath the truck.

Something seized his right arm, then his left bicep.

And something else bit into his throat, shearing his carotid. In a dreamlike haze, he remembered nearly drowning out at Black Lake when he was a kid...as he gagged on mud and his own dark, pulsing blood.

7

G*lub-glub-glub.*
More of the vile black drainage dropped into the sink. There was a good five or six inches of it in there now. Tessa did not believe it was all coming from the tap. Much of it, in fact, *most* of it, was gurgling up from the drain.

Though that was hardly her biggest concern.

Because there was something in there and it was alive.

It had not moved in the past ten minutes or so that she had been staring at it. She was beginning to seriously wonder if she had imagined it all. Maybe she had. Maybe—

There was a gurgling sound from deep within the black slop. It roiled and splashed, a few bubbles rising to the surface and popping one by one. Tessa stood there watching it, nearly transfixed. Her throat felt dry and her limbs felt weak. She wanted to get away from whatever was in there, but she seemed to lack the strength.

More gurgling.

A chunk of something about the size of a steel wool pad bobbed to the surface. It seemed to have the consistency of solidified grease. Whatever it was, it was disgusting.

Her stomach shifted unpleasantly.

It was times like this that she really missed Charlie, though she supposed she missed him just about every hour of every day. Tessa was old-school. If there was a creature in the house, then it was the man's responsibility to do something about it. She had no problem with traditional duties. The cooking and cleaning had always been her department—last thing she'd ever wanted in a kitchen was a *man*—and the fixing, sprucing, and creature-killing had always been Charlie's.

But Charlie had been in the ground these long seven years.

Tessa knew she'd have to handle this, whatever it was. The idea sickened her. Last year when the mice came to visit, she could barely keep her stomach down when she removed their broken little bodies from the traps. Somehow, whatever this was, she figured it would be worse.

The slop moved again and this time it was from the motion of whatever was in there.

Tessa felt faint with panic.

Perspiration beaded her brow.

She could hear people outside, calling to each other from porches. They were like shipwreck survivors shouting to each other as they clung to bits of wreckage. They couldn't help her.

If you want this critter out of your sink, old woman, then you're going to have to do it. Nobody but you.

Gah. The idea was appalling. The only thing that gave her strength was that the monster was in the sink, in the kitchen, and the kitchen was *her* domain. She trucked no interference from intruders here.

A weapon.

There was a bag of old plates and utensils she was sending to Goodwill. She plucked a roasting fork out of there. It was nearly as long as her arm and would do quite nicely. If what was in the sink had come up through the drain, then it was small. It would be no match for the roasting fork.

But just to be sure, Tessa dug out a tenderizing mallet. With the fork and the mallet, she was armed like a medieval knight.

All right, whatever you are, I'm ready.

She wasn't and she knew she wasn't, but there was no choice. Trying to keep her stomach down, she prodded the floater with her fork. Just the motion of doing that disturbed the slop and ripened the already horrendous gaseous odor emanating from the sink. It made her think of dead, waterlogged things afloat in stagnant ponds.

She prodded it again.

It looked very much like a piece of greasy meat, though stained darkly from the muck soup. Clenching her teeth, she jabbed the fork around in there and felt the tines scraping off the bottom of the sink.

Maybe there wasn't anything in there after all.

She jabbed around in there a few times.

Something moved.

She felt it brush against the fork, making waves of revulsion roll through her. She withdrew the fork…but, *dammit*, this was *her* kitchen! She was not going to be scared off by some stupid fish or whatever had swum up the pipe.

Getting angry, Tessa jabbed the fork around in there until… until with a physical shudder she felt it pierce something. Something thick. It felt like she had speared a summer sausage. It had the same sort of resistance to it as the tines went in.

Meaty was the word that popped into her mind.

Whatever it was, she had it. The crazy thing was, if it indeed was alive, then why wasn't it moving? Shouldn't it be squirming with pain or something?

Sucking in a breath between clenched teeth, she lifted the fork. The thing was weighty, a few pounds at least. She pulled it up out of the soup before she could change her mind.

What she saw made her freeze.

It looked like a snake. That's what she thought in an instant of absolute atavistic terror. It was maybe two feet long, but swollen, thick-bodied, big around as a can of beer. It was coiling with slow, oily undulations, dripping copious amounts of inky slime.

With a cry, she dropped it.

It splashed into the muck…and came right back out like a rocket.

Tessa had enough time to hold her arm up to protect her face before it hit her, the roasting fork dropping from it and clattering across the floor. It seized her wrist in its mouth, clamping down with a savage biting/sucking pressure and she clearly heard her wrist bones snap like twigs.

First she screamed.

Then she went wild with hysteria.

Barely staying on her feet, she spun around, waving her arm up and down and to both sides in an attempt to dislodge the thing. And as she did so, she felt more agony in her wrist. It was not just biting, it was *chewing*. Raging and flailing her arm, just wild with panic and pain, she managed to throw the thing. It thudded against the face of the cupboard, leaving a nasty brown-black stain like a splattered turd, and then dropped, hitting the breadbox and rolling off onto the countertop.

It was not moving now.

Just sort of vibrating, trembling.

Tessa looked down at her wrist and nearly went out cold.

It had eaten right through her skin to the muscles and tendons below. Blood ran down her arm, dyeing her hand red. She heard it striking the floor: *plop, plop, plop.*

She staggered and swayed, feeling light-headed. Whether that was from shock and trauma or loss of blood, she did not know. She tried to stay on her feet, to keep conscious. She knew that everything depended on what she did now. Stumbling over to the stove, she pulled a towel from the bar and wrapped her wrist in it, then wrapped another around it until it was swaddled like a baby.

But the blood...dear God.

It was all over her. It was on the floor. There was a crazy whorl of it on the wall, spattering the needlework GOD BLESS OUR KITCHEN hanging. There was dark irony there and she knew it. She had to call an ambulance before she bled out.

The muck...the muck in the streets! They'll never get through it... not in time.

No, but her neighbors. The Desjardins, the Mackenridges... she'd seen them out on their porches watching the flooding mud. They would help her. But she had to get to them.

She started toward the kitchen doorway, her slippered feet crunching over the remains of her mother's tea set.

She began to feel woozy right away.

Her mouth tasted dry and sweet.

Her vision was blurring.

Oh, she was feeling it now and more than just her throbbing wrist. She was seventy-seven years old and she'd been jumping around like she was fifteen. Her back was filled with needles, her knees aching, and her left hip felt like it might pop out of its socket at any moment.

The phone.

She fumbled it from its cradle, leaving a bloody smear over the stainless steel face of the oven. She leaned against the counter above the dishwasher. She thumbed a few buttons. *No, dammit, try again!* But she couldn't make her mind focus. For the life of her she couldn't remember anyone's number. The O'Connors. Yes. Just up the block. Their number was scribbled on the edge of the dry-erase board. She had bought Girl Scout cookies from their daughters.

The phone was picked up right away.

"Fern," Tessa managed. "Help me...I've been attacked..."

The phone slid from her bloody fingers.

The thing wasn't on the counter by the sink anymore.

God, where is it? Where is that awful thing?

A dirty black trail led across the counter, past the spice rack and right over to—

It was less than six inches from her right arm.

It was no snake, she saw that much now.

A huge, fat-bodied worm that was reddish brown in color, finely segmented like a millipede, and completely eyeless...yet it seemed to be looking at her. Its rear section coiling and uncoiling, the anterior end rising like a rattlesnake preparing to strike.

Tessa took all this in within microseconds.

She saw the forward segment of the anterior end pull back like a set of lips, revealing a gaping maw that was pink as bubble gum and set with rows and rows of hooked teeth that were sharp as roofing nails. They were stained with her blood.

This was what she saw.

The worm made a hissing *th-th-th-th-th-th* sort of sound.

Then it vaulted up and bit into her face. The next thing Tessa knew, she was on the floor and the worm had her. As it bit down again for a better hold, the liplike segment rolled back even more and the teeth slid farther from the gums like a shark chomping down on meat until Tessa's face was firmly impaled.

She was barely conscious by that point.

Moaning, groaning, trembling...but little more.

From somewhere distant, it seemed, she could feel the teeth digging in deeper, chewing and chewing, and the enormous suction of the worm's mouth as her left eye was sucked from its socket with a moist popping noise.

There was no pain. Just the gulping, slobbering sounds of the worm itself as it fed on her.

8

"Pat?"

Kathleen looked back toward the truck in the driveway. She saw the sluicing river of muck surrounding it, but nothing else.

"Pat?"

Maybe he'd stepped around the other side. It rose so high on its frame that she wouldn't have seen him. It was silent out there save for the gelatinous sound of the pooling mud flowing and sloshing. She swallowed, trying to make sense of things.

She had her back turned to him.

She was going into the house to gather up baby Jesse and whatever else she could throw together in the precious few minutes it would take Pat to back the truck up to the porch. She grasped the doorknob, let herself in...and then she heard a sort of grunting sound like he'd been kicked in the stomach, followed by a splashing.

When she'd got back out there, Pat was just...gone.

Filled with an electric, hysterical energy, Kathleen jogged down the steps and into the muck, nearly losing her footing in the slippery goo. It smelled even worse when she disturbed it, hot and gaseous.

"PAT?" she cried. "PAT? *PAT!*"

He was nowhere to been seen and she instantly switched into panic mode. The only possible explanation was that he had slipped, fell back and struck his head against the truck and gone under. There was only about three feet of the muck, but it was more than enough to hide a body. The stuff wasn't like water...it was thick and stagnant like river mud. He might not have floated to the surface as easily as he might have in water.

Don't freak out. Don't waste time, but definitely don't freak out. Do what you have to do calmly, quickly, and efficiently.

She heard the words in her head, but they were completely

lost on her. She dropped into the fetid muck on her knees and felt it seep into her pants and begin to fill her boots. It was not cold, but unpleasantly warm like something living. Frantically, she dug around through the goo. If he had indeed hit his head, she would feel him in there. He had to be right next to the truck.

But he wasn't.

As she dug around, practically flailing at the muck now, its polluted stench filling her head and nearly making her giddy, she shouted out, "OVER HERE! I NEED SOME HELP OVER HERE! PLEASE!"

Not ten minutes before, people had been clustered on porches and now there was no one. She dug around by the truck, reaching beneath it even, nearly breaking the steaming surface of the muck with her face.

Pat wasn't there.

He just wasn't.

On her hands and knees, she crawled through the filth around the other side of the truck, crying out and sobbing. She dug and pawed around in the muck and then she looked up at the truck itself. It was white, pearl white, but now there were bright red rivulets running down the passenger door like an immense amount of blood had splashed against it and was only now draining away.

Oh my God, oh my God.

Kathleen dug around, searching for something, *anything*, her voice not crying out now, but breaking in her throat and coming out as a disjointed and pathetic whimpering.

Wait.

She felt something.

She gripped it.

Pat's arm?

It felt about as big around as his lower forearm, though oddly soft and almost squishy. She yanked it up out of the muck and it was not Pat. It looked…covered in the black, dripping material… almost like an eel. It twisted and writhed in her hand.

She dropped it with a cry.

Then something bumped into her hip.

Kathleen pulled herself to her feet with the aid of the truck, leaving muddy handprints down its length as she escaped around the other side. She felt something brush against her boot. She stumbled to the porch, slipping and falling in the muck more than once.

She pulled herself up the steps.

She heard a slopping sound behind her.

Don't look back there. Whatever you do, do not look behind you because you'll see it—

Oblivious to her own good advice, she turned and saw the arched length of something about the size of a python rise from the mud sea and then submerge again. Like a shark showing its dorsal, she knew that whatever it was, it was coming for her now. Just as it had come for Pat.

9

Eva Jung lay in bed and waited for the end of the world the way she used to wait for Leonard to make love to her. It was a strange thing to think of and particularly now with Leonard having been gone all these years. But, maybe, as her final hour approached, it wasn't that unusual for a woman's heart to return to romance and things sweet and hot and long gone as the summers of her youth.

The years are leaves and they blow away one by one until there's not a single one left in the yard.

Eva knew that the National Guard and police would never get to Pine Street. There were 5,000 people in Camberly and by the time they got organized and started rolling, it would be much too late for most everyone. She knew this because the sun was beginning to set and then it would be dark. And dark was when the monsters came out. She knew that very well. Maybe as an adult she had tried to pretend otherwise as all adults did…it was easier to sleep at night that way…but she'd always known it was true. Tonight, the monsters would get into every house and kill every man, woman, and child.

It would not be a dark night like the nights always were in the stories her mother told her as a child. No, the moon would be up, it would be luminous and fat and brilliant. The stars would be out, winking long-dead light like diamond chips.

The better to see you by, my dears. The better to eat you by.

Eva thought of her neighbors. She had heard many screams already and she would hear many more by the end of the night. But she would not listen. People would die horribly as she would die horribly and it would be none of her affair. Her neighbors avoided her and that was fine. She held no grudge over it. She was a woman, not quite old at fifty-three but certainly not young, who lived alone in a big wind-trembling house that creaked and rattled at night.

What would they say to her even if they were to talk to her?

How does it feel, Eva, to be all alone in that big house with nothing but yellow memories for company, your husband long dead, and nothing to listen to but the screech of a hoot owl on the rooftop late at night? She was glad they didn't talk to her so she wouldn't have to answer that. Because if she did, she would have told them it was awful, simply awful to wake up at three in the morning and reach out for the strong shoulders of your husband and find only emptiness. It was awful to be lonely and listen to your own rising anguish as tears spilled hotly down your cheeks.

But tonight, she was not alone in her suffering.

The neighborhood suffered with her.

They would die together and perhaps, just maybe, be reborn into a better place that was free of suffering.

She listened to the muck flooding into her house and the slitherings of the monsters in the pipes. They would make themselves known soon and she would be waiting for them as she had once waited for Leonard. She would accept the death they brought with open arms because death was painful like love and true love was resurrection.

10

Two doors down from Eva Jung, Bertie Kalishek pulled off a Lark 100 and said, "Ah, that's because you haven't lived through the crap I have. You're just a kid and you, my dear, do not know crap. Hell, you don't even know what color it is or what it smells like."

Donna Peppek sighed.

She was beginning to debate the logic of waiting this out with Bertie. Bertie was good for the most part. If you could get past the chain-smoking, beer-guzzling, and near-constant reminiscing about older, better times. Some days Donna enjoyed her, some days she did not.

This was turning into one of those days.

Donna had gone over there because the idea of waiting this out alone was unthinkable. They kept saying on the radio that the National Guard were evacuating the town street by street, that everyone needed to sit quiet and wait. If there was a medical emergency, they were to call 911…but *only* if it was an emergency. Other than that, they advised staying out of the muck.

Don't have to tell me twice, Donna thought.

Between the constant Emergency Broadcast System bulletins on the radio, Bertie's grating voice, and the clouds of pungent smoke, Donna was getting a first-class headache.

You know you didn't want to come over here. You wanted to go see Geno.

Which was exactly why she came to Bertie's. The idea of being in the house with him *and* Ivy was simply too much. Donna had been avoiding Ivy in every way possible…something that wasn't too hard given Ivy was practically a shut-in. But being in her house and having to talk with her and interact with her…no, that was just too much.

Maybe fucking her husband wasn't such a good idea after all.

Donna sighed. The guilt, the guilt, the guilt. It haunted her constantly. Yet, for all of that, she could never say no when Geno stopped by. Now wasn't that just something?

"...so you better believe me when I say I haven't felt anything like this since," Bertie said.

"Since when?" Donna said, realizing she had completely tuned her out.

"Since the Cuban Missile Crisis. I don't think any of us that lived through it will ever forget it. We were god-awful close to doomsday. Awful close. Those were two long weeks for the world, I tell you." Bertie butted her cigarette. "I remember it well. That's when I stopped smoking L & M and switched to Lark. Been with 'em ever since."

To prove it, she fired up another.

"I hope they get here quick," Donna said.

"Who?"

"The National Guard. I want to get out of here."

Bertie laughed. "Don't be naïve, honey. We won't be first. Not over here. The Guard will start over on the north side, that's where all the rich yahoos live. They'll get to us, but I bet it won't be for hours."

Donna peered out the window at the rising muck. "We don't have hours."

"Sit down and have a beer." Bertie popped a fresh one and toasted her with it. "Way I see it, if this is doomsday and we're all going to die, piss on it, might as well face it drunk as sober."

11

---

*P*laying possum.

   That evil little motherfucker was playing possum.

   That's what the worm had been doing, as absurd as it sounded, and Tony knew it. If he doubted it at all, there was an utter conversion of faith when the shit pipe exploded like a mortar tube and a gushing eruption of brown-black filth sprayed into the air like a sewage fountain. It covered Tony and knocked him on his ass. It sprayed up the walls and splattered the ceiling and flooded the floor. Like a hemorrhaging artery, it kept leaking, sending a surging river of muck out into the living room that washed right over him and pushed him three feet back with its rollers.

   "Jesus H. Christ!" he cried out, sitting up as the discharge kept flowing out of the bathroom, thick as syrup, warm and glopping like vomit.

   Tony tried to climb to his feet, slipped and fell, madly brushing it from his face. A banner of toilet paper was hooked around his boot, a turd rolled off his lap as he scrambled to his knees. Drenched with piss water and just about everything else from the sewers, he gagged at the stench, dry heaves convulsing his stomach.

   On his hands and knees, it was no longer dry-heaving but the real thing. He spewed out some bile until he was panting and gagging. Stevie stood there watching him. He was skinny as a drowned rat now that he was drenched in the muck, a streamer of toilet paper around his throat like a necklace.

   Tony almost laughed at him, but he knew he looked worse.

   This was just a fucked-up nightmare from beginning to end.

   There was well over ten inches of the percolating, bubbling goo on the floor. *Wait until Charise gets a load of this.* The stink of rot and methane made his head swim. He had to get out of there before he was completely overcome by the fumes.

   And the worm, dummy, don't forget about the worm.

But he didn't have to worry about that because just as the thought passed through his mind, the worm rose from the muck in the bathroom. Though it had no eyes, it directed its nodulelike head in his direction, a low, barely perceptible vibration coming from it.

Stevie started yipping at it right away.

The vibrating got louder. The entire worm was trembling with it, sending out tiny ripples through the muck. Its segments were pulsating. The head opened like the bulb of a flower, peeling back to reveal all those teeth that looked like shards of the sharpest bone. There was no denying that this thing was designed by nature to grab and hold on, to tear into flesh and glut itself on blood.

Very carefully, very quietly, Tony began to get up, keeping his eyes locked on the worm.

Stevie had stopped yipping now.

He was leaning forward on three legs, the fourth cocked like a Pointer. Tony grimaced. This was a hell of a time for him to begin acting like a real dog.

"No, Stevie," he said in almost a whisper.

The dog began to growl low in his throat. Of all things. Tony had never, ever seen him act this way. The worm was a threat and he was becoming territorial, drawing on some long-submerged instinct.

The worm was hissing now, gouts of fluid hanging from its mouth.

Stevie began to inch forward, stalking slowly.

"Goddammit, Stevie! Stop it!"

The dog was about four feet from him. He knew Stevie very well. That dog was very fast when he needed to be. Tony had a very ugly feeling that if he tried to grab him, he'd go racing right at the worm to engage in combat that he would never ever win.

Stevie stalked forward.

Tony knew he needed a weapon. Any old thing would do. Just something to throw at the worm to distract it, to buy him enough time to grab the dog and make it out the door.

"*Stevie*," he tried again.

It was pointless. Stevie was completely territorial. He was overwhelmed by atavistic genetic memory, channeling his evolutionary ancestors and their primal, savage need to protect what was theirs and destroy any and all invaders.

Goddamn dumb mutt, now's not the time!

The worm's hissing was very loud.

It accepted the contest and was ready to fight. It was a thick-bodied thing, only now it was even thicker, having compressed each coil until it looked like a very fleshy, mucus-dripping Slinky, its mouth wide, jaws extended, teeth like a ring of spikes.

Tony reached for the first thing he could find that had any true weight: a James Patterson novel in hardcover lying in Charise's rocking chair. It was thick and heavy. He had read a Patterson once at Charise's bidding and quickly went back to Elmore Leonard. If he could peg the worm with the book, then he would quickly change his opinion that Patterson's books were of little use except as doorstops.

He got his hand on it, hefted it...then with a shrill barking, Stevie launched himself right at the worm.

"STEVIE, NO!"

The dog charged in and the worm did not move until he was well within striking distance. It waited there like a coiled spring and when Stevie came in for the kill, it moved...it rocketed forward like one of those gag snakes in a can. Its bunched and compressed segments released their muscular pressure and it shot out at Stevie like a bullet, moving with the same blurring corkscrewing motion it had used when it drilled through the wicker clothes hamper.

Stevie literally exploded in a Technicolor blur of blood, bones, and tissue.

The worm punched right through him in an eruption of red, scattering his remains in four directions. The dog had time to let out one pathetic squeal before he was disemboweled and nearly turned inside out. Meat and blood spattered the bathroom walls, tufts of hair drifting down like pillow fluff.

"STEVIE!" Tony shrieked as the worm bored through him.

Then it was coming for him, spinning like an ice auger and he threw the James Patterson book. It hit the worm dead-on, knocking it to the side and into the muck, the book nearly torn in half by the time it fell.

By then, Tony was running.

He grabbed his softball bat and went slipping and sliding through the living room, knowing the worm would be coming for him now and knowing he didn't stand a chance. His best escape route was through the kitchen so that's where he went. With any luck—*gah*—the worm would feed off Stevie and that would buy him some time.

Nearly drunk with terror and fear, he launched himself out the back door, flying right off the porch into the muck where there were far worse things waiting.

12

When Ivy screamed—and she screamed absolute bloody murder—Geno jumped out of his chair on the porch, nearly broke his ankle tripping over the stoop, barked his hip on the door frame, and scrambled into the kitchen swearing under his breath.

He had no idea what he was going to see.

But by the time he got there, he was pissed off.

Ivy was backed up against the wall by the table. She had a rolling pin in her hand, of all things, and it was raised to strike like some incensed housewife in an old movie, preparing to brain her husband.

The floor was flooded in the black mud. There was only maybe an inch or two at most where he was standing, but over near the appliances and particularly in front of the sink, it was at least a foot deep.

"Holy oh shit," he said. "What a fucking mess."

The doors under the sink looked like they'd been nearly blown from their hinges and that's where the stinking muck had come from: under there. It had flowed and sprayed in gouts, by the look of it. And that left only one possible explanation. The waste pipe had burst.

These were the things he saw within his first few seconds of entering the kitchen. It was ugly and smelling and a real mess, but none of it, of course, explained Ivy, who looked like she'd just found a head in the refrigerator.

"It's under the sink!" she said. "Right under the fucking sink!"

Geno just looked at her. "What's under the sink?"

It seemed like a perfectly rational sort of question, but it was lost on Ivy. She could only stare in the direction of the sink itself, moonstruck, her eyes swollen in their sockets, unblinking and bloodshot, a sheen of saliva on her chin. She still held the rolling pin high. She was absolutely frozen with it like some kind of classical Greek sculpture…sans the rolling pin, of course.

He was going to ask her again when one of the doors under the sink swung shut with a thud, dangling from its hinge. The other one was jammed, it seemed, halfway open.

Well, whatever it was, it was still in there.

Right away, Geno figured it was a rat. What else could it be? If the waste pipe had burst, bringing that sludge up with it, then it wasn't that surprising to him that it might bring a rat up, too, from the sewers below.

A weapon was what was needed.

He saw the broom in the corner. Better than nothing. The handle was stout and heavy, more than enough to brain a fucking rat and especially one that had been shot up from the sewers in that tidal flow of muck and regurgitated under the sink.

"Geno…don't…" Ivy managed.

But by that point, he was pretty much ignoring her because she looked like she was completely losing it, shaking and quaking, eyes wide and blanked with fear, a string of drool hanging from her lower lip. She was a mess, not that he was surprised. It didn't take much to strip her gears; they were already worn precariously smooth.

This was a man's job, Geno figured, and he would handle it, the way he handled most things with a wife that lived in a near-constant state of progressive mania. When the phone rang, she moaned, thinking somebody had died. When a car she didn't recognize was parked across the street, it was criminals casing the joint for a robbery. The ache in her left arm was certainly an oncoming major coronary. Kids walking by were dealing drugs. When a chain letter came in the mail, there was a conspiracy being launched against her. Christ, she rarely left the house anymore because she was afraid of a) catching some horrible communicable disease like bird flu, and b) that she would be beaten and raped in the parking lot of the Piggly Wiggly.

That one always made him laugh. *Sure, hon, they might try to rape you, but they'll never finish. Take my word on that one. Fucking you is like fucking an ice cube tray.*

Not that he would ever have said anything so cruel, crude, and degrading like that to her…even if it was true.

Which is why you stop by Donna Peppek's house twice a week.

But he didn't have time to be thinking of the guilt involved in that or the sheer joy of Donna herself. Friends with bennies, that's all.

"Geno…don't do this."

"Don't worry. I'll bash its head in."

She licked her lips, shaking her head. "It's a worm."

A worm? Is that what she fucking said?

Jesus, this was good. He was arming himself for a first-class rat battle when all he needed was a boot to step on it with. He went over to the sink and used the broom handle to pry the door open.

He heard a gurgling sound.

It sounded like an upset stomach. That's what flashed through his mind very quickly and then…then both doors flew open and a gout of black, syrupy fluid spewed out in a frothing surge, spraying over his shoes and fouling his pant legs. It looked to be equal parts shit, mud, and black subterranean gunk. It splashed to the floor in a spreading, steaming pool. It was as if the cupboard had vomited on him.

"Fuck," he said under his breath.

And it was as he said this that he saw two yellow eyes staring up at him from the darkness under the sink. He took one step backward and jabbed the broom handle at whatever in the hell was under there, which was certainly no rat and couldn't possibly be a worm. The broom handle did not hit it exactly, it skated off it like it was greased.

He saw then that what was under there did not have yellow eyes at all.

In fact, it had no eyes. What he had seen was the overhead light reflecting off it. But that brought him precious little comfort as the thing came out, striking at the broom handle like a pissed-off water moccasin…only it was no water moccasin, but a monstrous shit-brown worm that was as big around as his thigh and looked to be about the size of a very large boa constrictor.

Geno stumbled back, slipping on the muck and falling on his ass as Ivy totally lost it and began to cry, "*Geno! Geno! Oh my God, get away from it, get away from it!*"

Which he knew, in the back of his mind, made perfect sense.

The doors slammed back shut as the thing retreated, or at least as shut as they could get in their condition, and he had a truly crazy idea that the worm had set up housekeeping under the sink and needed a little privacy. That was insane. But that's exactly what passed through his mind in those few seconds of peace right before the worm came out again like a snake from a rabbit hole, taking one of the doors right off its hinges and rising up above him like a serpent that was ready to strike.

Ivy really let go with a cry then.

She dropped to the floor on her knees, wailing with the sound of a mind that had been torn right open.

Geno had been afraid of very little in his life, but as the worm hovered over him, dirty brown, dropping clots of black muck, its bullet-shaped head moving from side to side in some obscene rhythm, he felt a very real need to crap his pants out of sheer terror.

He drove himself away from it, scuttling on his ass over the floor.

He thought the worm would strike, but it didn't.

It kept moving its head back and forth on its neck…hell, it was *all* neck…and Geno would have kept backing away in sheer primal horror and revulsion, but his shoulders made contact with the face of the refrigerator. The worm had allowed him a bit of backward scuttling, but he seriously doubted whether it would let him turn and crawl the six feet he would need to get out of the fucking kitchen.

And he couldn't just abandon Ivy to that monster.

The hell you can't—she's already abandoned herself.

But that was the kind of thing a coward would say to justify his actions, Geno knew, trying to prove to himself that he didn't have a slit between his legs after all.

The worm moved right past Ivy as if she was inconsequential, just a shivering white bag of neuroses and that's pretty much what she was. It zeroed in on Geno because it knew that's where the action was. Geno wouldn't go down easy and maybe it sensed that.

Geno watched it come, playing possum, which wasn't too hard because everything inside him—from bones to muscle, tendon to ligament—had gone to pudding now. The worm was composed of multiple segments, each covered in a membranous, glistening red-brown flesh that looked nearly pulpous. They seemed to move independently of one another, inflating and deflating as if they were breathing, exuding a viscous mucuslike slime as it pulled itself forward over the floor. Each was set with fine, wiry bristles that dug into the tiles and pushed it along with a scraping sound like forks scratched over tabletops.

Geno knew nothing of worms.

He did not know that what he was looking at was a gigantic, monstrous annelid like a rag worm or a leech or that the flexing, convulsive roll of its segments was due to a type of *ditaxic* locomotion caused by the extension and contraction of its muscles. He only knew it was a monster. When it got close, close enough to raise its head off the floor, he saw the forward segment peel back like parting lips from a circular fleshy pink mouth as large as the opening of a coffee can. It was filled with rows of hooklike teeth that would have been called specules in a tiny worm, but looked more like shining hypodermic needles in this beast. They were set in spongy gums that seemed to jut two or three inches from the mouth itself.

He saw what looked like droplets of venom drip from the teeth.

A grayish slime hung from the mouth in ropes.

That god-awful mouth was the most horrible thing he had ever seen in his life and within seconds, he knew, it would be on him, those teeth peeling his face right from the skull below.

So he did the only reasonable thing: he swung the broom. And it was no girly, limp-wristed, halfhearted attempt, but a double-handed swing that would have popped a ball right over the stadium fence.

Whack!

He put all his strength and weight behind it. He was almost sure it would take that fucking worm's head right off, but that's not what happened. The annelid primarily consisted of liquid and it took the blow like a water balloon might have—when the broom handle knocked its neck (for lack of a better word) aside, lacking bony structures, it merely *squished*, then burst with a gush of sewer-stinking fluid that sprayed against the cupboards.

And as Geno watched, the fore and aft segments merely closed the gap left by burst one.

It can't die! Can't you see that? You can't beat it to death!

But damned if he wasn't going to try. As the head came back around, he made it to his feet and swung the broom handle, knocking the worm back and away. The mouth peeled open, hissing at him, and he clearly felt the slime spray against his face like spit. Some of it got into his left eye and it burned. He blinked it away and swung at the worm, kept swinging. Knocking it hard this way and that, fluid spraying around the kitchen.

It was getting pissed.

Its segments were ballooning, the mucus oozing from them in a brown, gushing foam. It coiled. It wormed. It bulged like a bicep.

But in the end it wasn't as stupid as he had hoped for.

Gasping, nearing the end of his strength and clearly no closer to victory or even to driving it off, he swung the broom handle, trying to brain it, to smash its head to sauce...but the worm had secreted so much mucus by that point the broom handle glanced harmlessly off it. No matter how he hit it and at what angle, it simply glanced off the thing as if it was coated with cooking spray.

With a last valiant effort, the broom handle once again skated over the worm...and flew from his hands.

Shit...oh shit...oh fuck...

The lips peeled back, the teeth slid out and Geno felt piss run down his leg as the worm darted at him, teeth slashing. He ducked out of its way once, then twice...then he tried to seize it in his hands, but it was like trying to take hold of a canned ham thick with aspic jelly...his fingers just slid over its bloated, slimed segments, its bristles cutting into the palms of his hands.

He thought it would bite him, tear his face off, but it didn't. The mouth closed and the bulblike head snapped forward like a fist, striking him in the chest and flattening him. The wind knocked out of him, he hit the floor, dazed and confused. It felt like his sternum had been split open like a dry sheaf of corn.

When he opened his eyes, the mouth was inches from his face.

The teeth were gleaming like scalpels.

A hot, toxic steam blew out of the worm's throat, coating his face with a greasy, rancid mist that stank of the sunless, necrotic, polluted holes it had crawled up from.

Geno managed a weak scream.

Then out of the mouth came a yellow, stringy tangle of thrashing cords that must have been tongues. The ends were sharp like tent stakes and they jabbed right into him. They went into his throat, his lips, they impaled his tongue...right away, he was numb. The worm had paralyzed him, anesthetized him and he just sat there, back against the fridge, limbs limp, eyes glassy and rolling in their sockets.

I won't feel it...at least I won't feel it.

And that was the best he could hope for. The head arched back and went right at his left kneecap, the teeth sliding from the pushed-out, glossy-pink gums. They pierced his knee like ice picks, sinking in a good inch or more. He was aware of the impact of the mouth, the pressure of the teeth…but that was about it. When his kneecap came off in a bloody spray of tissue and ligament, he felt only the pulling and the snapping, but none of the pain. In fact, he didn't even realize his knee was gone until he saw the beast spit it from its mouth in meaty, clotted mass.

It was as it went for his face that Ivy started to shriek.

Then she attacked it.

13

Kathleen stumbled into the house, slamming the door shut behind her.

Filthy from the muck, tears welling in her eyes, her entire body shaking, she dropped onto the carpet, hugging herself, absolutely manic with terror.

I saw it. Outside in the muck, I saw it. A snake. A giant snake. It must have gotten Pat. It must have killed him.

These were the words that kept rolling through her mind and she couldn't seem to stop them. They came unwanted and unbidden, hammering home the very thing she feared most: being alone. Alone with some horrible serpent even then circling the house, looking for a way in.

She had to breathe.

She had to get control.

She couldn't come apart like this.

She brushed tears from her cheeks, leaving dirty streaks of warpaint on her face. Standing uneasily, swaying from side to side, she stumbled into the living room and grabbed the cordless and dialed 911 after two or three tries in which her fingers simply would not cooperate.

When the 911 operator answered, she let it out in one mad torrent: "My name…my name is Kathleen Mackenridge…I live at 2112 Pine Street in Camberly. The mud is flooding us…my husband was killed by a snake…a giant snake…it came out of the mud…"

The 911 operator, obviously used to hysterics, said quite calmly as she had been trained: "Ma'am, listen to me. I want you to relax. Emergency services have been activated and neighborhoods are being evacuated even as we speak. Stay indoors. The mud is not expected to rise much higher. In fact, it may—"

"DID YOU HEAR WHAT I JUST SAID?"

"Ma'am, I realize that—"

"YOU DON'T REALIZE SHIT!"

"Ma'am, please, you really have to—"

"LISTEN TO ME, GODDAMMIT!" Kathleen shouted. "MY NAME IS KATHLEEN MACKENRIDGE AND I'M AT 2112 PINE STREET IN CAMBERLY! YOU GOT THAT? GOOD! MY HUSBAND IS MISSING! I THINK HE WAS KILLED BY A GIANT FUCKING SNAKE THAT CAME OUT OF THE FUCKING MUD! YOU GOT THAT? NOW WHAT THE HELL ARE YOU GOING TO DO ABOUT IT?"

There was silence for a moment. A crackle of static. "Did you say 'snake,' ma'am?"

Kathleen realized at that moment she was very, very close to an absolute nervous breakdown. She was crying. She was dirty. She was getting black muck all over the goddamn carpeting. Her heart was trying to slam its way out of her chest and her scalp was trying to crawl right off her head. And this idiotic bitch was not listening. She was just not fucking listening. Kathleen had a mad, almost itching sort of desire to break out into laughter over the absurdity of the entire situation.

"Ma'am? Are you there?"

"YES, I'M STILL FUCKING HERE! I'M TRAPPED IN THIS FUCKING MUD! MY HUSBAND HAS DISAPPEARED! I THINK A SNAKE GOT HIM! WHERE IN THE MOTHERFUCK DID YOU THINK I WAS GOING TO GO?"

"Okay, ma'am. Now here's what I want you to do," the operator told her, addressing her like she was a melodramatic seven-year-old. "First, I want you to sit down and take a deep breath and then I—"

"FUUUUUUUCK YOOOOOOOUUUUU!" Kathleen screeched, throwing the cordless as hard as she could at the brick fireplace hearth and nearly squealing with childish joy when it shattered into a dozen pieces of cheap, Asian plastic.

You're on your own, you're completely on your own, a voice in her head told her in no uncertain terms. *What you do, you'll have to do for yourself. So, first off, do not fucking sit down and take a deep fucking breath. Go directly upstairs and get Jesse. Lock yourself in with him. Get Pat's shotgun, load it. Call Marv or Tony or Donna or Geno or somebody. Get the neighbors over here. Now…move!*

She grabbed a fireplace poker, turning a blind eye to the framed photographs on the mantel of her happy, little life with her happy, little husband and son and mother and friends…all of which had become very unhappy by this point.

Feeling so wired with hysteria and fear she thought she might short-circuit at any moment, she stumbled over to the stairs, gripping the railing and trying to breathe, trying to get some oxygen up to her head before she blacked right out.

She couldn't go on like this.

Jesse had slept like an angel through the whole thing, but he would sense it on her the way babies always can. They're hardwired to their parents' emotions. She had to put on a brave, calm front. Whatever else she did, she had to manage that…some how or some way…

Except there was something dark circling in her head.

Something very wrong.

Then she knew what it was.

Jesse.

Jesse never sleeps this long.

No, no, no, no, no…not that…

Kathleen jogged up the stairs and charged down the hallway, making it nearly halfway down its length before she stepped in the oozing black muck that had flooded out from the bathroom. Her feet went up in the air and she came down hard, smacking the back of her head on the hardwood floor.

When she opened her eyes, it could have been two minutes later or twenty minutes for that matter. Her vision was blurry and unfocused for a moment or two, her mind slowly sweeping the cobwebs away. She was lying in a pool of the horrible inky drainage, sopping wet with it. It had coagulated and clotted around her like thickening, wet concrete.

She sat up, her head spinning. There was a dull throb at the back of her skull.

God, she was covered with the stuff.

Jesse. Get to Jesse.

She pulled herself to her feet. She saw that the bathroom was nearly drowned in muck. It was dark and slushy and smelling. A slimy trail of the stuff led down the hallway toward the door at the end which was Jesse's room. *The nursery,* as Pat's mother had called it.

Oh God no…

Grabbing up the poker, she ran down there and charged

through the doorway, praying, hoping, calling out for any god that would listen to help her, help her now. It had never been so important. She made it maybe three steps through the door when she tripped over something, going down face-first, her poker clattering across the floor.

What is that...what did I trip over...something soft...

As she pulled herself up, she saw with grim and fateful clarity all the black slime on the crib, how it dripped and ran down the spindles and dropped to the floor—*plop, plop.*

Kathleen screamed and raced over to it, gripping the side as she looked down in there and saw...nothing. It was empty. The crib was completely empty, save for the black filth all over the baby blankets and bumper pad, something that looked like a foul mix of mud, seeping rank water, and moist black clotted leaves from the bottom of a pond.

As the scream cycled out of her mouth and the room seemed to spin round and round, her heart thundered in her chest and her own breathing sounded like wheezing bellows in her ears. The room was dimming as the sun set and her face was rinsed of color. She felt the blood drain out of her head and trunk and down into her lower extremities. Darkness filled her brain and she dropped to her knees, devastated by fright, completely senseless. This was the aftereffect of absolute horror, of looking the worst-case scenario dead in the eye.

How much time passed before she was able to move or process even the simplest rational thought, she didn't know. Shadows were beginning to crawl across the floor. The light coming in through the blinds was negligible.

She began to move.

She had to turn on the light and proceed very calmly now. A voice in her brain was giving her the same pep talk as when she went to look for Pat. She knew beyond a doubt that something very dirty and hideous had come into this room and snatched her son. She did not know what it was, but her mind kept telling her it was the snake that had gotten Pat.

Now it was in the house.

It was in *her* house.

It had killed her husband and now her infant son. Though part of her wanted to rage and scream, she did neither. There was no point in screaming. Screaming was to vent horror and to bring help, but there was no valve that could release the horror inside of her and no help to be found.

What she would do, she would do alone.

The snake was here somewhere and she would find it.

There was nothing left inside her now but the need to hunt the thing and bring about its doom.

Yet, for all her hate and all her resolve, she sank to the floor, sobbing...at least until her mouth opened and a wailing voice came out: *"WHERE'S MY BABY? WHERE IS MY BABY?"*

14

Eva Jung lay on her bed, not asleep and not quite awake, thinking, dreaming, wondering about arteries and veins and capillaries. These are the words she used even though she knew what she was really thinking about were *pipes*. All the pipes that connected the town to the freshwater pumping stations and the wastewater treatment plant. An absolute network that united homes and factories, office buildings and apartment houses as arteries, veins, and capillaries connected organ systems into a common whole.

Wasn't that funny and wasn't that strange?

In came the water and out went the waste, just like a living thing. The good, clean water came up through narrow pipes and aqueducts, all the bad stuff was sucked below into subterranean channels of night and dank brick catacombs where rats scratched and things bobbed in rivers of filth. It all went down there—the piss and shit, gray water and bacon lard, hairballs and menstrual blood, old spaghetti and animal fat, all the rotting waste, the vegetable and animal matter, the organic detritus of human kind.

Down there, down below, down in the black, diseased, and reeking bowels of the city.

And it was there, she knew, that things mutated and took shape in the sunless, polluted, steaming channels and pipework. Oh yes. The very same things that were rising now and spilling into the streets and homes on bubbling rivers of black muck.

Knowing this, Eva decided the veins and arteries of the town were more like conduits that linked the dark underworld with the sunlit world of men. They were highways that led into every single house.

15

In the end, Marv O'Connor left Fern with the kids because there was no damn way he was letting her go out into the darkness with that goddamn reeking mud flowing in the streets. Fern weighed about 105 pounds soaking wet. He could just picture her getting washed away in the slop never to be seen again. No, this was a job for someone a little meatier and that was him. At 6'3" and 260 pounds, it was going to take some real mud to wash him away.

Besides, he was just as worried about Tessa Saldane as she was.

Help me…I've been attacked…

Those were the words Fern said Tessa used on the phone. Marv knew Tessa pretty damn well by that point. She wasn't someone to call and say something like that unless there was a very real threat. She was far too old and far too proud for such theatrics.

But *attacked…?*

It was crazy.

It was no easy thing getting over to her house. Tessa lived at the very end of the block and that was a long, slow slog when the muck was up above your thighs. Marv was wearing his rubber chest waders or he would have been soaked to the skin with the filth which was not just mud and muck but sewage as well, judging by the vile stink of it.

After a good twenty minutes of chugging along, he finally got to Tessa's.

He dragged himself up the porch and pounded at the door. His legs felt weak and weightless after pushing through the mud for so long.

"Tessa!" he called. "Tessa! It's me, Marv O'Connor!"

There was no response. He threw the door open and charged in, calling her name and clicking on lights as he went. He got a bad feeling right away and wished he had brought something to defend himself with. Even a penknife. Anything. All he had was a flashlight.

It was the smell in the air that bothered him.

It wasn't the gaseous, noisome stench of the black muck, but a smell that he was all too familiar with as a deer hunter: blood. The house was a ripe, reeking envelope of it. It smelled the way the gut shed up at hunting camp smelled in November...like a slaughterhouse. The stink of bowels and marrow, animal fat and oceans of draining blood.

But here...in Tessa's house?

He moved faster until he reached the kitchen. Then he came to a dead halt as he reached for the light switch and clicked it on. The smell was so bad in there, so concentrated, that it brought his stomach up the back of his throat.

Then, in the light, he saw.

Tessa was dead. In fact, she was more than dead. She looked like she had been torn right open. She was lying in a pool of blood, more of it splattered against the counters and smeared on the cupboards and appliances.

Marv turned away.

When he turned back, something moved.

What the fuck?

It crawled out from beneath Tessa's corpse, parting her hair like a comb...a worming, fleshy thing that seemed to be composed of ringlike segments, each of which seemed to be pulsating. It looked like some kind of millipede. More so, like some flesh-eating nightmare worm from a B-movie. It crawled free of Tessa, hitting the blood-puddled floor with a soft thud.

Then it raised its anterior end off the floor and showed him a perfectly oval cavity of a mouth with perfectly sharp teeth.

It hissed.

Marv took two shuffling steps backward, his hand blindly—and instinctively—reaching out for some kind of weapon, because he had no doubt this thing was a fucking killer. Maybe it was only two or three feet long, but it was thick around as his arm, muscular and evil with teeth made for shredding. His fingers fumbled across cutting boards and canisters of flour and salt.

The worm lowered its head/mouth back to the floor.

It began to vibrate. Then it began to move in his direction... slowly, slowly, but he had the oddest feeling that if it wanted to, it could fly right across the room at him with dizzying speed.

The butcher block. He yanked a carving knife free.

The worm came at him, not slowly now, but with amazing speed. He knew he could have dashed through the door, but the idea of turning his back on that monster was scary. He could just about imagine it climbing his spine and sinking its teeth into the back of his neck.

It leapt.

It was four feet away and Marv was brandishing a carving knife that could gut a pig, still it leapt...fearless, remorseless, almost manic with its need to attack. It made it to within a foot of him before he swung the blade and missed, his wrist knocking the worm to edge of the counter where it hung, the spiny protrusions jutting from its segments scratching to gain a hold.

Marv let out a cry and slashed at it with the knife.

He missed the head (if *head* it could be called) and slashed open a couple of its segments that pissed out a vile, watery discharge that could not possibly be blood. The worm turned to fight. It struck at him and he slashed it again, laying it open. It made a weird trilling sound that might have been a cry of pain.

It knew then he was dangerous.

Like most predators, it was basically cowardly. Fattened and sluggish from feeding on Tessa, it wanted to kill, but it wanted an *easy* kill. So as he hacked at it again, it fled. It slithered over the counter with great speed and unstoppable power. It knocked aside dishes, overturned the flour canister, and slid behind the breadbox when he stabbed at it. Then it jumped up and clung to the underside of the cupboards when he brought the knife around.

It oozed copious amounts of foaming brown slime that left a dirty, greasy trail behind it. The fluid practically gushed from its segments.

Marv knew what it was trying to do.

The sink was full of black muck and that's where it had come from and that's where it was going now. It was retreating with a full belly. It did not want to fight; it wanted to hide.

It moved, it slinked, it slithered and wriggled.

He kept slashing at it, making damn sure it knew he meant business so it would not get any bright ideas in its little wormy brain and decide to counterattack. He had to keep it on the defensive.

When it reached the sink, it turned and bared its teeth, hissing again.

The mouth darted at him, the segments elongating so its strike was fast and elastic.

Marv kept away from it, only slashing at it when it pulled back.

It tried to get into the left basin of the sink where the black goo was still bubbling and slopping. He slashed it, cutting it open. It tumbled into the right basin, twisting and writhing, its spines scraping over the shiny metal trying to get some kind of a grip and finding it nearly impossible.

Marv struck.

He brought the knife down and speared it just behind the head, slime and brown goo flooding the basin in a discharge of jelly. The worm hissed and flopped, but he had it and he knew it. But he wouldn't have it long. He had it pinned to the sink, but he could feel its strength. It was flexing like a huge muscle, pulsing and straining, pouring out mucus, its body inflating and convulsing.

It would work itself loose and he knew it.

Kill it, kill this motherfucker!

"No, you don't," he said under his breath as its whipping tail tried to wrap around his wrist, its spines tearing open the back of his hand. He turned on the garbage disposal, the Insinkerator, and it began to whir and gurgle, a few bubbles of black goo coming up out of the drain cup.

The worm fought manically.

But Marv was determined.

He forced it into the drain, pushing it down with the knife until he heard the blades bite. The worm went stiff like a penis, throbbing and straining, then loose and limp and whipping. The Insinkerator blades chewed into it. He used his free hand to shove the bulk of the worm down into the drain.

More goo came bubbling up...but this was pink and meaty with foaming slime. The Insinkerator kept whirring.

Finally, Marv shut it off.

He stumbled away, refusing to look at the remains of Tessa and refusing to think about what had just happened.

16

Snarling like an animal, Ivy launched herself at the worm.

Geno saw her do it, but he was numb and helpless from worm toxins and the loss of blood. It was all like a dream to him. He was beyond the point where he even knew what day it was or where he was or how he had come to be there.

Ivy seized the worm with a murderous fury and tore it away from his knee. She gripped it right behind the head with both hands like it was a poisonous snake and right away, the worm began to writhe and squirm with muscular contortions and boneless gyrations. It was a powerful, sinuous creature that did not like to be grabbed. Its fanged mouth hissed, its head segment snapped from side to side, its body looped, but she held on with impressive strength and determination.

"*You fucking thing!*" she shrieked at it. "*You don't come into my fucking kitchen with your filth and disease!*"

The section she gripped seemed to sag and deflate.

The worm had a hydrostatic skeleton pressurized by fluid. The tighter she gripped it, the more the fluid was drained into other segments. But that hardly meant it was going to submit without a fight. Its body began to whip in her hands with violent contractions, the segments oozing out a thick, gelid mucus until she could barely hang on to it. They flattened. They elongated. They swelled with fluid.

It was like trying to hang on to a high-pressure hose.

Ivy did not give in.

Even though its bristles cut into her fingers like pins, she increased her hold, gripping different segments. The mucus made her hands slide from segment to segment as the muscles of the worm contracted and relaxed in fluidic waves.

Its tail flailed wildly, knocking things off the counter and she was thrown this way and that by it. Its body curled around her with a crushing embrace, its thorny bristles digging into her skin. Then its head slid free and Geno, through dimming eyes, saw its pulsating length coiling around his wife, the segments fattening with hydrostatic pressure until there was the clear sound of things bursting inside her, ligaments popping and bones dislocating.

A moaning sound in his throat, he reached out one flaccid hand in her direction.

But by then, the worm had already torn off her right arm like a chicken wing with a gristly, grinding noise.

17

Tony stumbled up the steps of Stephani Kutak's house, breathing hard and reaching for the doorbell. *Doorbell? You're really going to ring the fucking doorbell?* The absurdity of that nearly made him laugh, but there was nothing very funny about it or anything else. Still, he knew he had no right to barge in without announcing himself, so he rapped his knuckles on the door a few times before letting himself in.

"Steph?" he called out. "Stephani? It's Tony from next door. Are you there?"

Maybe she was hiding.

Maybe she was freaked out.

She was an attractive woman who lived alone and it would only make sense that she might be a little on edge. The whole damn neighborhood was on edge and with good reason. Tony stood there, dripping muck onto the carpet, wondering how Charise was faring downtown and how she would take the news of Stevie's death.

Stupid fucking dog. I never liked that dog...not much anyway.

But he wasn't going to think about Stevie. He refused to go through it all again. His real worry was what had *gotten* Stevie. There were things in the muck and he had a nasty feeling that the worm that had gotten his dog was not one of a kind.

He stepped farther into the house.

In his fantasies, he'd been invited into this house again and again, but it had never once been like this.

"Steph?"

There was only silence...heavy, brooding, and thick with something very much like menace. There was every possibility, of course, that she had escaped when the mud started filling the streets. Yet, for some reason, he just didn't believe that.

"Steph? Are you here?"

He nearly shouted it and his voice echoed throughout the house, bouncing down hallways and through empty rooms before coming back at him with the tonal quality of a scream. Maybe it wasn't that bad except in his imagination, but there was a quality to it he didn't like, one that was quite nearly hysterical.

He reached around on the wall until he found the light switch.

Better. The shadows were swept away. He crossed the living room and turned on the hallway light and that's when he saw the slimy, muddy trail that led across the floor into the kitchen. Something in him sunk at the sight of it. It didn't necessarily mean there was a worm in the house. Maybe Steph went out into the muck and tracked it back in herself. Maybe.

He stepped cautiously, very cautiously down the hallway with nothing to defend himself with but the softball bat. He was trying hard not to think about what had torn Stevie apart, how very deadly and relentless it was. How it punched holes in doors and turned wicker hampers to sawdust and drilled right through one silly, harmless dog who, in his last moments, had decided to be a dog and defend his turf and maybe, just maybe, had been defending something of a little more worth.

That goddamn mutt was trying to protect you and you know it. He died trying to kill that fucking worm because in the final analysis, you were his master and he would have done anything for you. That's loyalty, my friend. Just try and find that in a human being.

Tony wiped his eyes. No more goddamn walks in the park. No more yipping. No more chewing up things. No more accidents. No more anything.

"Dammit, Stevie," he said under his breath.

The situation was getting the better of him and he had the strongest desire to just sit down on the floor and cry. He fumbled in his shirt pocket for a cigarette, lit it with trembling fingers. *Lookit me, Steph, I'm smoking in your house. What do you think of that, Little Miss Perfect?* He felt almost guilty doing it, knowing how fastidious she was about everything. She kept her little house as perfect as she kept herself. She never invited anyone into either. She never let any hands but her own touch those things she loved best. That was funny, too. Good-looking woman like that with no men (or women for that matter) in her life. She had a few female friends—Charise had been one of them—but that was it, and to call them *friends* was kind of stretching it.

Acquaintances, Tony thought. *She never had anything in her life but acquaintances.*

Maybe she was afraid of sex, afraid of commitment, afraid of relationships in general…and maybe she loved herself so much that the idea of sharing herself with another made her jealous.

Tony pulled off his cigarette, staring at the muddy trail.

The floorboards upstairs creaked momentarily. Houses made noises sometimes, he knew. Nine times out of ten, it was nothing. He went over to the stairs.

"Steph?" he said, his voice echoing and dying.

He heard no more sounds and that's why he knew he had to go up there, even though the fear rising in his gut warned him against such an idea.

Nobody could really blame you for leaving now. You tried and she's not here. You really have no right to track this stinking mud all over her house, so go over to the O'Connors', wait this out with Marv and Fern. Or visit Kathleen and Pat. Go see Geno. He was drinking beer on his porch not that long ago. Don't just stand here, do something.

But he wasn't going to go to the O'Connors' or the Mackenridges' or the Desjardins'.

He was going upstairs.

As he climbed them, he said, "Hey, Steph, it's me Tony from next door. There's some shit going on you have to know about, so I'm coming up to tell you about it. If you're naked…well, that's a chance I'm willing to take…"

He blabbered on and on, whistling past the graveyard, until he reached the landing above and then his mouth simply closed in midsentence. It closed like a trap. It was like a switch inside of him had been thrown. There was something in the air. Something ominous and nearly overwhelming.

The hallway was dark.

Very dark.

He had to feel along the wall for a light switch and he was almost certain that long before he found it, something would find him…some dark, twisted, elfin shape would come hobbling out of the darkness, reaching out for him with knobby fingers.

Click.

Light. That was better. There were no grinning horrors waiting in the shadows. In fact, there was nothing but an ordinary hallway. There were three doors. The first two were wide open.

One was Steph's bedroom—the garden of delight—and the other a guest room. He was interested in neither. He went over to the closed door. It was the bathroom. He knew that from his one visit two years before when Steph had thrown a birthday party for her sister.

"Steph?" he said, rapping on the door. "You in there?"

He knew somehow she was. It was as if all the energies of the house were gathered in this one place, behind the closed door. The last thing he wanted to do was catch a peek of her on the toilet, but if she wasn't aware he was in the house by now then it meant she was in trouble.

Tightening his grip on the bat, he opened the door and pushed it in.

In that brief moment of darkness while his fingers fumbled for the light switch, he heard a wet, sliding sort of sound he knew was not good. Then the light was on.

"Oh, shit, Steph," he said, turning away.

But when there was absolutely no response from her, he turned back. She was sitting naked on the toilet, her long legs spread, her back up against the tank, her head slumped forward. Her eyes were open and staring. They looked like green crystalline pools.

"Steph?"

He wanted very badly to think he had merely caught her in mid-dump, but the truth was much worse and he knew it. Black muck had slopped up from the toilet and spilled to the floor. Globs of it had run down the inside of her legs. There was blood on her lips.

She was dead.

There was no doubt about it.

She was dead and he knew it.

Then she started to *move*.

Her eyes still wide, green and glassy and unseeing, she wavered from side to side like she might fall right off the pot. And it was as she did so that he heard a moist, tearing sound that was coming from *inside* her. She began to lean forward like she was going to stand up and pitched right over at his feet...a swollen, monstrous worm sliding out of her in all its segmented, blood-slicked, phallic horror.

He stumbled back in the doorway, nearly going down.

The worm had been eating her from the inside out. She was

facedown on the floor, the bloody globes of her ass still raised as if in offering to that obscenity.

It raised its head at him, the forward segments pulling back and opening like a pipe to reveal the mouth and its rows of hooked teeth. A slime of blood and mucus rained down to the floor.

It hissed at him.

And Tony ran.

He did not think; he ran. He darted down the hallway and tripped down the steps. Then he was at the door, falling out into the night, so devastated by what he had seen that he could not even scream. He didn't stop moving until he heard something moving through the muck in his direction.

18

I'm coming for you, motherfucker. I'm coming to kill you. I'm going to beat you to death.

Clutching the fireplace poker in her white-knuckled fists, Kathleen stalked the thing that had slid into her house like a vein of shadow. She would find it. She would kill it. Then…then…then… then she would go quietly mad because she wasn't too far away now. Maybe not in the same house, but definitely living next door.

The trail of muck was easy enough to follow.

If the creature—*snake, had to be a goddamn snake, a fucking python*—was trying to practice stealth, it was failing miserably. It was about as stealthy as a shit-leaking pig. That was the comparison that leaped into her mind and she almost screamed because that's exactly what Pat would have said.

Don't you dare fall apart. Not yet.

Trembling, sweating out hot/cold beads of perspiration, she followed the muck trail, turning on lights as she went. The trail led from the bathroom to Jesse's bedroom. Where was that fucking thing and where was her baby?

She tensed.

She heard a low, rolling rumbling sort of noise just as she had when this whole nightmare started. The house shook. It shook again. The rumbling grew louder. The house moved and she went down on her ass in the muck again as ceiling tiles cracked and jagged rents opened up in the walls. She could hear things falling and crashing downstairs. She was certain one of them was the picture window.

The house is falling down.

She scrambled to her feet in the oily black filth and jogged down the hallway to the stairs. She did not know where she was going. She did not know what she would do when she got there.

Her brain was moving, it seemed, in every direction at the same time. And what was behind it, what was fueling it was not the loss of Pat or even that damn snake but something bigger, something vastly more important: *the baby, the baby, the baby…where is the baby?* All she could see was the baby. She was hypercharged with maternal need to protect her child, only she did not know where her child was.

Move! Do something! Do anything, but you must find the baby!

The words made perfect sense, but she did not know what to do. Her animal instinct told her to find that fucking snake and kill it, but her maternal instinct told her all that mattered was finding her child. The rest could be sorted out later.

She had to search the upstairs.

That's what she had to do.

And this was exactly what she was going to do, but the rumbling started again and this time the house trembled like a dog had seized it and shaken it. She reached for the railing, but lost her grip and went tumbling down the steps, *thud, thud, thud.*

The house continued to move.

Everything was in motion. The floor seemed to be rolling beneath her the way they said floors did during earthquakes. The lights flickered. They went out, then came back on. The walls were cracking open, coughing out clouds of plaster dust. The dining room ceiling caved in, crashing down onto the antique cherry wood table. It hadn't been the picture window she heard, but the kitchen window. No matter, the picture window now followed suit. The parquet floor shifted, buckled, the individual blocks pulling apart. The ceiling fan came crashing down.

Then the house began to bleed.

At least, that's what it looked like. Oceans of dark, bubbling blood oozed up from the cracked, disrupted block floor.

No, not blood…muck.

The same sewer-stinking filth that was in the streets and had vomited from the upstairs bathroom.

My house, my fucking house…it's coming apart! It's all coming apart!

Kathleen sobbed. Her body shuddered. Something had let go in her brain now. And even though she was far too gone to realize this, she still felt the sense of loss, the sense that there was a great and jagged division between the here and now and what her life had been only a few hours before.

On her hands and knees, she began to crawl as the house moved with occasional tremors around her. She crawled through the muck that bled from the floors, moving from the living room into the trashed dining room and kitchen beyond. Ghost fingers of dread slid along the nape of her neck, trying to warn her away from the muck and what might wait in it, but she was oblivious to just about everything by that point.

Still clutching the fire poker, she stopped.

She cocked her head and listened intently like an animal.

She could hear pieces of the ceiling still dropping. Water running. The muck dripping. But she wasn't interested in any of that. She was listening for the reptile that had come into her house and taken her life away from her. She would kill it. There was nothing else left in her mind but the desire to kill the thing.

It was here.

She knew that much.

If she kept listening, she would hear it sliding from room to room, stalking her…an evil serpent, its form reticulated and silent, its triangular head set with glittering green eyes, raising even now to strike—

There!

Her breath caught in her throat as she heard something soft and large drop to the floor in the living room the way a boa constrictor would drop on its prey from a jungle tree. Yes, it was coming for her, thick-bodied and serpentine, seeking her out in the semidarkness. It would not show itself until it was certain of the kill. It slithered forward, winding through the muck, closer and closer.

Kathleen stripped her coat away so she could fight unimpeded.

Closer. It was almost visible now.

She tensed, bringing up the poker.

She could see it now…its spiraling shape rising up and up. It knew where she was and now it would strike. With a cry, she swung the poker at it, striking it with a fleshy impact that threw stinging fluid in her face. Had it spit poison at her? Her eyes were burning. She pawed the stuff away with her free hand and it felt like cool jelly. She swung the poker again but something happened. It didn't strike the thing so much as glance over it, more jelly spraying into her face. The poker slid along its oiled length and out of her fingers. She heard it clang to the floor.

The snake made a hissing noise and came right at her.

Before it could bite her, she seized its neck in her hands. Its touch was repellent. A big snake was supposed to feel smooth and rippling with muscular contractions, but this thing was soft… almost gelid. Her stiffened fingers actually pierced its flesh. It was pulpous like the brown spots of decay on a rotting apple. Every inch of it seemed to be crawling and greasy, fluid gushing over the backs of her hands. It had spines that cut into her fingers like the thorns on a rose stem.

It was no snake.

It was a worm.

An immense, semigelatinous worm. It was thicker around than a beer can, seeming to swell by the moment. It writhed in her grip like a fire hose under high pressure. It slid through her fingers and she couldn't seem to get a grip on it. It was like trying to take hold of a rubber tube greased with bacon fat. It moved. It squirmed. It twisted with corkscrewing undulations.

Then it was loose.

Its obscene weight fell in her lap and it attacked immediately. She thought it would go for her face, her eyes, or her throat. But it did none of these things. What it did was much more appalling: it brushed between her legs like an immense and flaccid penis, then darted its head upward, sliding under her hoodie and up over her belly, the bristles of its skin tearing into her navel. Its swollen length slid between her breasts the way her husband once had.

The effect was nauseating.

Her breasts were heavy with milk and the worm seemed to know it.

She cried out, falling on her ass in the black slop. She yanked and pulled at the worm but it looped in her fingers, thick gouts of foaming slime issuing from it. She could not hold it or tear it away. Its mouth flexed open, shearing through her bra, and enveloped her left breast. She screamed. Its mouth was cool. She could feel its teeth scrape against her like piercing needles. She beat at it, her nails cutting trenches in its flesh, but the teeth bit right into her.

Kathleen let go with a wild, shrieking cry.

The worm's teeth slid into her breast, impaling deep into her mammary glands, bringing forth blood and warm milk as the ducts were pierced. She fought all that much harder, but the teeth held on. The mouth shriveled to a puckered hole, suckering to her nipple. She could feel its length pulsating as it drained her with unbelievable pain. It was like being hooked up to a milking machine. The real agony was not that, but when it tore her nipple loose from its intense, vigorous suction.

At the same moment it did, its teeth lost their traction and she yanked it free, jerking it out from beneath her hoodie and tossing it across the room. She was doubled over with incredible, devastating waves of pain, her hoodie soaking red with her blood.

But the worm was not done.

It was coming to finish her.

It slithered through the muck and vaulted at her. She snatched its writhing form in midair with two blood-spattered fists. She squeezed it, trying to tear it apart, but it was elastic and fluid. Then with a manic cry, she brought it up to her mouth and bit into it, her teeth rupturing its membrane. This, combined with the force of her hands pulling it in opposite directions, sheared it. She bit it in half, her mouth filled with an eruption of gurgling slime and gushing worm jelly.

She went over, vomiting, emptying herself. The heaving was agonizing with her injured breast. Before she passed out, she knew she had to get free, she had to get out of the house.

She ran stumbling out the door, leaving the wriggling worm sections behind her. Screaming and sobbing, she waded out into the thigh-high muck that bubbled and coursed around her legs… vile, yet almost soothing with its warmth.

There was something floating out there.

"My baby," she said picking it up. "*My…baby…*"

19

Tony tried two more houses in the neighborhood and found destruction. Not just the destruction from the muck and the houses themselves coming apart, but destruction from the worms that had tunneled into each and every one of them like maggots into bad meat, feeding on what they found there.

As he slogged through the muddy sludge in the streets, he heard screams from time to time.

What kind of fucking nightmare was this?

He was just glad Charise wasn't here. He hoped she was safe. The worms were using the muck as a vector, he knew, to bring them to their prey, and it was working pretty well thus far. The city streets were supposed to be man's turf. It was his element. But the muck had changed all that and what had once been familiar and safe was now deadly and alien. The muck was swimming with monsters. Like sharks in a sea of blood, they were circling, closer and closer.

Which is why you need to get to shelter. You have to find somewhere they can't get you or you won't last the night.

But where was that? An attic? A roof? The mud was still rising and safety was beginning to become something of an abstract term.

He had to relax. He had to get somewhere safe, but he couldn't panic in the process because if he panicked, he would make mistakes. And if that happened, the worms would take advantage of it.

One of these houses had to have people in it.

People he could stand and fight with.

Tony stopped as he heard a splashing sound and ripples moved through the mud sea. Something was out there. Something was moving beneath the surface and it could only be one thing. He needed to move but it was the thing he feared most. Instinct told him to run *and* it told him to stay still. The worms weren't the brightest lights on the tree. Very skilled predators as far as that went, but not real smart. If he moved, they would seek him out. If he stayed still, they might pass on by.

Carefully, very carefully, he snaked a hand into his hoodie and dug his cigarettes out of his shirt pocket. He lit one and dragged deep off it.

See? See how fucking calm you can be when you have to?

Pulling off his cigarette, he waited there, still as a post.

Now and again, there were ripples around him. The muck roiled, splashed. Eventually, there was nothing. He sighed and let his back slump.

It was then he saw a form moving in his direction.

20

Death would be love's last enduring kiss, Eva Jung decided. It would come in the night and its lips would be the heat that lit one last fire in the cooling embers of her heart here on this darkest of all dark nights in this bed where her husband had once made love to her.

The neighborhood was coming apart out there. She could hear houses crashing and walls falling and roofs collapsing. Her own house shook. Its foundation cracked open, black muck filling low places like dark arterial blood, pooling and shifting and ever rising. She could hear pipes bursting and looping forms sliding down hallways and up stairwells.

But she was barely even aware of it. She felt only the years pressing down on her and the emptiness that described them which was hollow and without form. She was lying under the sheets, naked, her flesh covered in a slight dew of perspiration— the sweat of fear *and* the sweat of anticipation. In her soul, she was a virgin untried, her overripened fruit unplucked and untasted but juicy and full. Soon, very soon now, she would not be alone.

She heard a sound out in the hallway beyond her partially open door: a secretive sliding like skin against satin sheets.

Leonard? Leonard, is that you?

Though she knew somewhere in the vacant corridors of her brain that Leonard was dead, still she waited for him and would not have been surprised if his dark shape filled the doorway. She could almost smell his cologne, which always reminded her of well-oiled leather and green, needling pine forests. What she smelled then, what filled the room in dark fumes, was not that but something else. Her breathing increased as the door swung open and she could smell the foul sweetness of her lover. He had come unbidden, hungry and virile. She would be his meat and his wine and he would grow drunk upon her taste, giddy with what she had to offer.

Bring me your love. Bring me the filth and dirt of it. Let me squirm in it.

Her lover approached the bed with that same satiny *swish-swish* that was pre-seduction. Her heart throbbed in her chest. Her breath came quickly. Her skin was prickled with gooseflesh. She could smell what had come to take her. Its stink filled the room with a gassy foulness of rotting drainage ditches, but she was unaware of it. She smelled only the cologne: pine forests and pipe tobacco and worn leather. Her madness here on this last night of her life was complete and seamless; dream obscured reality and fantasy shrouded fact.

Please, oh God, please don't make me wait, please...please...

Though she was hardly aware of the fact, Eva had uncovered herself, exposing her secrets to her lover. She spread her legs so he might enter her. Her lover raised his head above the level of the bed. Eva did not dare look upon him and destroy the beauty of these precious last moments. It was Leonard and she believed it was Leonard. To look upon the obscene, glistening foulness of the ichor-dripping thing that had come for her would shatter the illusion and it had to remain whole. So she refused to look at the immense, bulging vermiform creature that hovered between her spread legs, its segments pulled back like a foreskin to reveal an enormous oval mouth and the circular rows of razored teeth hanging with caustic threads of slime. Droplet by droplet, she felt its saliva burning hot against her sex.

Now...make it now...

Her lover did. Spinning with a corkscrewing motion indicative of its species, it entered her with a cutting, terrible velocity that brought blood and searing agony as she was torn open and ruptured, sinking into the bed which became a soup of her own fluids. She screamed and screamed again, dying with a last perverse taste of wickedness as she was quite literally split in two, knowing death was surely love's last enduring kiss.

21

Kathleen moved out into the muck, unable to smell the steaming rottenness of it anymore. It seemed the world had always stunk like this. In the tight, crowded confines of her mind, she was unable to remember a world that was not flooded in bubbling black sludge. She stood there watching it, feeling it moving around her with tiny, sluggish currents.

"Don't worry, baby Jesse," she said, "Mama will get you out of this. One way or another."

Weak from the loss of blood, she blinked away the dizziness that made her world pitch this way and that. She had to concentrate or she'd never get them out of this. Luckily, the baby didn't weigh much.

She moved forward, being very careful of where she placed her feet. It wouldn't do to slip in the muck now.

Sobbing, she clutched the baby tighter to her breast even though the agony of doing so sent white jolts of pain through her. But that was okay. The pain kept her conscious and kept her moving.

She wondered if anyone was left in the neighborhood.

She saw a few lights, but that didn't mean anything.

"Okay, Jesse, Mama's going to keep walking until she gets us somewhere."

Kathleen didn't know where that would be because so many of the houses on Pine Street were coming apart now. But she had to keep looking because it wouldn't do to have Jesse out in this and, by God, she needed to sit down.

Moving with the stiff-legged locomotion of an automaton, she moved forward into the mud sea.

22

At the O'Connor household, Fern waited.
She waited in the kitchen, peering out into the darkness.

Marv's been gone an awful long time, she thought as she stared down into the drain, wrinkling her nose at the smell coming up which was enough to curl the hairs in her nose. *He should have been back by now.*

There was no point in calling over to Tessa's. She'd already done that three times now and there was no answer.

Fern didn't know for sure what she was afraid of, but the fear would not leave her. It existed inside her, cold and slow-crawling, casting a shadow over her rational mind. There were a lot of things that could have happened. Marv could have been washed under and drowned. That seemed unlikely because he was a very sturdy, strong sort of man. He could have been overcome by the gases. But again, that didn't seem plausible either. The houses in the neighborhood were coming apart and he could have been caught in a fall of wreckage. The only thing that had saved their house thus far, she figured, was that it was made of brick and would have probably outlasted the others by many decades if not a century.

When Tessa called earlier, she claimed she had been attacked. *Attacked.* But by whom or *what?* This was what Fern feared most, that whatever had gotten Tessa had also gotten Marv.

Oh, why hadn't he taken his rifle with him?

Fern listened to the girls in the other room. They had uplinked their Nintendo DS systems and were having some kind of war. They were laughing, teasing each other, squealing with joy and growling with derision. Kids were really something. They could adapt very quickly. Thank God the Internet was still working or they'd have to play a board game or (gasp) read a book.

Barbaric, perfectly barbaric.

The smell coming out of the drain was getting worse.

So bad it made Fern almost woozy.

"Well, there's only one cure for this," she said under her breath. She went into the broom closet and came back with a jug of Hilex bleach. There wasn't anything down there bleach couldn't handle.

At least, she hoped not.

23

It was Tony that found Marv after Marv staggered out of Tessa Saldane's house, the carving knife still in his hand.

"Hey," he said.

Marv clicked on a flashlight and aimed the beam directly in his face.

"Jesus," Tony said, covering his eyes.

"Who...*Tony?*" Marv breathed. "What're you trying to do? Give me a heart attack?"

"Sorry."

"I guess we're all on edge tonight."

"Yeah." Tony swallowed. "Ain't that the truth?"

"I'm glad you're still kicking."

"Neither of us'll be kicking long if we don't get out of this slop."

They trudged side by side. After a time, Marv said, "The worms?"

"Yeah."

They exchanged stories quickly. There was no beating around the bush. They'd both seen them and there was no doubting the reality of the things. The hows and whys would have to be hashed out later.

"Have you checked out any other houses?" Marv asked.

"Yeah. They're either empty or...well, they're not empty and nothing's alive in them."

They took a breather after a few minutes, the muck wearing them down. It was like wading through molasses. They leaned against a light post, gripping it like they might get sucked away.

"What are we going to do?" Tony finally asked, dragging off a cigarette.

Marv sighed. "We'll get back to my house. We'll hole up there with Fern and the kids. We find anybody else, we bring 'em in with us. I've got some guns, camping equipment in the garage if we need it—lanterns, flashlights, a cookstove. We should be all right."

It seemed reasonable, Tony figured. As reasonable as anything he'd heard lately anyway. Together, they might have a fighting chance while they waited for the National Guard and emergency services. He was going to say just that when Marv grabbed his arm.

"Somebody's coming," he said, listening to a slow, dragging splashing moving in their direction.

24

As Fern poured the bleach into the sink, the most amazing and shocking thing happened: something came worming its way out of the drain with a bubbling, foul-stinking black goo. And *worming* was the right word, she realized, because what came slithering out was indeed a worm.

Not a snake, as she first thought.

A fucking *worm*.

She jumped back and nearly dropped her bottle of Hilex. As it was, she cried out low in her throat and if her lips hadn't been sealed tight it would have been a scream. *What in the hell is this? What the hell…*

The worm came up out of the drain with a convulsive, dying shudder, twisting and writhing. It was about as long as her forearm, but thick in body, fleshy and absolutely disgusting. It flexed with violent muscular contractions, a jellied ooze pouring out of it in a snotty tangle. How something that big around fit down the drain in the first place was beyond her.

The only good thing was that it was not only in considerable pain, it looked like it was dying.

"Mom," Kassie called from the living room. "Are you all right?"

"Mom?" Kalie echoed.

Shaking, a fine dew of fear-sweat on her brow, Fern realized if she did not unglue her mouth and speak right now, the twins were going to come in and they were going to see what she was seeing and she simply could not have that.

"Ah…yeah, I'm fine. Just cleaning the sink."

The sound of her own voice gave her a modicum of strength and she stepped a bit closer to the sink. The worm was barely moving by that point. *What if I hadn't poured the bleach down there? Would it have stayed in the drain or would it have come out after me?* The questions jumped into her mind and she ignored them.

She poured more bleach onto the worm.

It moved sluggishly and spewed out something like several yellow and tangled, ropy tongues. But as revolting as that was, what was even worse was that it was steaming. The bleach was doing something to it. It was deflating and breaking apart, decompressing into a puddle of slime.

Trying to keep her stomach down, Fern forced its remains down into the garbage disposal with a long wooden spoon and turned it on. She listened to it whir and chew at the remains while a bubble of bile slowly rose in the back of her throat.

She shut the disposal off.

Then she stood there, dazed and sickened, wondering if she had hallucinated it all.

25

Kathleen saw the two men out in the mud sea, but she was barely even aware of their existence. They might as well have been stumps. She was driven by one single overwhelming need and that was to get Jesse away somewhere safe.

When she got close to them, one of them reached out and stopped her. "Hey...*Kathleen?*"

She pulled away, snarling at them. They were not going to get the baby. She would kill them if they tried.

"Kathleen...easy now...it's me, Marv. Marv O'Connor."

She tried to make sense of this, but her mind was like a blender on puree: a great, ever-spinning mix of emotions and impulses. It took her a minute. Finally, she cocked her head like a dog. "Marv?" she said in a broken voice.

"Sure. Tony's here with me. You know, Tony Albert."

"Hey," Tony said.

She just looked at them blankly. She could not connect the names with the faces, but slowly, slowly it started making sense to her. She swallowed, then swallowed again. "I can't find Pat and my house is falling apart and I have to get Jesse somewhere safe." She kissed what was in her arms. "Somewhere the worms can't get us."

Marv and Tony looked at each other.

"Well," Marv said. "You better come with us. We're going over to my house. It's safe there."

Kathleen hugged her baby and nodded. *Safe.* She liked that word. That was the word she wanted to hear and a place she wanted to go. Making a low humming in her throat, she followed along behind them as the blood continued to drain from her wounds.

26

"One foot in front of the other," Donna told Bertie. "That's all we have to do. It's only two doors down."

"Maybe that's nothing to you," Bertie said, "but when you're my age, that's a goddamn long way, missy."

Donna had to give her that one. The mud was deep and it was like trying to wade through porridge. The fact that she had gotten Bertie out of her house in the first place was a minor victory. All they had to do was make it down to the O'Connors'. On an ordinary day, it was a two-minute walk. In this muck with a frail, stubborn old woman with her, it was like the Bataan Death March: endless.

Bertie almost fell again, but Donna caught her and held her up.

"See no reason for any of this," Bertie said. "Could have stayed at my house. I knew this was a bad idea. I knew I shouldn't have listened to you."

And your newfangled ideas, Donna thought. She was just waiting for Bertie to say that like some cantankerous curmudgeon in an old movie, Walter Brennan maybe. The idea made her smile.

"We couldn't stay there, Bertie. The place was falling apart."

"Like hell it was."

Donna decided she wouldn't argue. They were over halfway to the O'Connors' and they were not about to turn back. The fact of the matter was that the house *was* falling apart. The muck had made it shift. A window in the kitchen had broken. And even Bertie couldn't deny that cracking noise they heard coming from the foundation.

"Just a little farther now."

Bertie snorted. "A little farther, my ass. We're going to die out here. Well, I got one up on you: I already have my gravesite bought and paid for. I picked it out ten years ago. All they have to do is carve my death date onto it."

She seemed very proud of the fact and Donna could only sigh. *What was that?*

Donna stopped them there in the muck. For a few seconds, she barely breathed.

A great rippling passed through the mud just ahead of them as if something quite large had moved beneath it.

"Well, what the hell now?" Bertie asked.

"Just wait a minute."

"I don't have a minute to wait. I'm near dead now."

Donna ignored her.

She heard the rippling again.

This time it was behind them. Now off to her right. It was like they were being circled by something under the mud. And as crazy as it seemed, the first thing that jumped into her mind was *shark*, even though that was perfectly ridiculous. Sharks didn't swim in mud and they sure as hell didn't live in fucking Wisconsin.

Yet…that eerie sense that they were being circled did not lessen. It increased.

Behind them, there was splashing…as if something had surfaced and then dove again.

"C'mon, Bertie, we have to get over there. It's not far."

"Isn't that what I've been saying?"

Donna tried to move faster in the mud, but that only got Bertie bitching at her all the more. They had to move fast. Donna couldn't explain it—and she sure as hell did not have the time to—but something out there was closing in on them.

Something very big.

Above, the full moon came out.

27

Tony wanted to pull Marv aside and say, *that's not a baby she has, that's not Jesse, it's a fucking plastic baby doll. Kathleen's carrying a fucking baby doll. Don't you see that?* But, of course, he didn't because he couldn't and he figured he really didn't need to; Marv was fully aware that Kathleen was crazy. And like Tony himself, he did not want to know the details of what had sent her wandering through the sludge with a baby doll.

Tony was thinking about Fern and the twins.

Did they really want to bring this crazy woman back with them? But then, what choice was there? They couldn't leave her wandering. Fern would know what to do. Women always did. Tony was almost beginning to wish Charise were there. Even Stevie.

But he didn't want to think about Stevie.

Kathleen had stopped.

By the time they became aware of it, she was fifteen feet behind them. She was just standing there, making a deep moaning sound that was nearly erotic in tone like she was quite near to getting off.

"Oh...oh...*oh*," she said in a voice filled with confusion and delight. "It's so warm. It's so very warm. Can't you *feel* it? It's almost hot. I can feel it all over my legs, all over my...my..."

"Kathleen," Marv said. "We have to go."

She just stood there, hip-deep in the muck that seemed to be rising by the hour, struck senseless like she was in some kind of religious rapture. Marv called out to her and she started moving again, very slowly, plodding along like she had been wound up with a key.

She stopped again, went stiff as a pillar. She looked like a toy soldier in the moonlight. "Oh...oh...oh," she said again. "It feels like it's boiling, like it's...it's..." She never got farther than that. Her mindless rambling became a gasp of surprise, then one of pain.

Her hand had been trailing in the mud.

She jerked it free and there was a worm hanging onto it. It was a huge, bristled monster that looked to have the circumference of a wastepaper can. It had bitten into her hand and now it bit it once again. Tony clearly heard the bones snapping under intense pressure. Kathleen whipped her head from side to side, screaming and flailing her arm, trying to rid herself of the thing, but it wasn't working.

"*Shit!*" Tony shouted out into the night. "*It's got her! One of those fucking things has got her!*"

He stumbled forward into the muck but Marv grabbed him, pulled him back. "No," he said. "You can't help her."

Tony was ready to swing at him.

He *could* help her, but he goddamned well needed to get to her first…but then the worm rocketed up out of the muck and this time, it swallowed her entire arm right up to the shoulder blade. It retreated just as fast, its teeth peeling not only the sleeve of her raincoat free, but her skin as well. It peeled her arm right down to red meat and tendons.

"KATHLEEN!" he cried out.

She disappeared beneath the muck.

By then, Marv was dragging him off and Tony just didn't have the strength to fight him.

Behind them, the muck roiled and sluiced and splashed upward in great foaming gouts. "*Help me!*" Kathleen cried out as she surfaced, her face black with mud. "*Oh dear God somebody please help me! IT'S GOT ME! IT'S GOT MEEEE—*"

She thrashed in the bubbling sludge, but was beyond help. Absolutely beyond it. The worm kept biting at her, taking more of her with each strike. Its teeth gleaming like surgical knives, it scraped across her chest taking not only most of her coat away but her breasts, too. Great segmented loops of it wound her up, squeezing her until her screams became a choked, gurgling sound. Her bones were crushed with a sound not unlike dry autumn leaves under boots. Her head thrashed from shoulder to shoulder like some grisly puppet, a gout of dark arterial blood ejecting from her between her lips with incredible hydrostatic force.

Then she went limp, her insides bulging from her mouth.

One bloody hand still slapping at the gelid flesh of the worm, maybe out of reflex action, it towed her under the surface. Both Tony and Marv could clearly see a slow-cresting torpid wave moving down the street as the worm dragged her away to unknown depths to be fed on at its leisure.

"C'mon, Tony," Marv said. "We have to go..."

But Tony just stood there, staring dejectedly back to where she had been in the muck. There was nothing there now, not so much as a ripple. No...there *was* something floating there and for one panicked moment he thought it might be one of her limbs.

But it was nothing like that.

Just the filthy baby doll floating on the surface of the muck.

28

Holed up in the O'Connor house were all the survivors of Pine Street: Fern and Marv O'Connor, Tony Albert, Donna Peppek, Bertie Kalishek, and the twins—Kassie and Kalie. As far as they knew, there was no one else. The mud sea outside was rising and soon it would be completely impassable. Marv figured if the goddamn National Guard didn't arrive real soon, things were not only going to get desperate but downright ugly.

But as Fern had said, they were together and they were alive.

That was true, he figured. Unlike the other houses on Pine, he knew his was much older and had actually been a farmhouse back when there were no other houses on the street (which was then just a dirt drive). The point being, it was solid brick and it had weathered a lot of years. So far, it was weathering the mud sea, too, unlike a lot of the other prefabs that had nearly completely collapsed. He figured they were safe. And Fern, God bless her, kept a very well-stocked pantry, so nobody would go hungry.

Donna Peppek was doing her best to keep Bertie Kalishek under control and Fern had engaged the twins in a game of Crazy Eights. This by candlelight, of course, now that the power was out. Something which made little sense, because the lights were on across the street. Go figure.

Marv went down into the basement with Tony and grabbed the lanterns from the camping equipment. They were battery powered, but that was no problem because like food and toilet paper, Fern had stockpiled them. When they had the living room lit up nicely, they went into Marv's little den at the back of the house and unlocked the gun cabinet. He had three weapons: a Mossberg four-ten, a bolt-action Remington 30-06 with a scope, and a .38 Special that had belonged to his dad. There was no ammo for the .38, but there were fifteen rounds for the Mossberg bird gun and ten for the Remington deer rifle.

They had food.
They had lights.
They had arms.
They were safe.

"I got this bad feeling things are going to heat up out there," Tony said as he loaded the four-ten.

Marv nodded. "Me, too. If it was just me, I wouldn't be too worried…but with Fern and the girls. I don't know. I'm scared."

"Let's go make sure nothing happens to them," Tony said.

29

The mud was moving out there.

Marv watched it through the picture window. It was no longer just slowly bubbling and oozing, now it was in motion. Huge, dark waves of it were cresting and splashing through yards and slamming into houses with considerable force. A wave of water was one thing, but a wave of mud had considerable weight behind it. As first one and then another hit the house, the living room trembled. The windows rattled. A painting fell off the wall. An anniversary clock on the mantel pitched to the floor and shattered.

"Everyone just hang on!" Tony called out.

Another wave was coming and it was much bigger than the other two. The only good thing about it was that waves of mud, despite their weight and force, moved very slowly. Marv told everyone to get behind the couch and brace themselves.

"Here it comes," Tony said.

Between the moonlight outside and the streetlight at the corner, it was fairly bright out there. The light glistened off the rolling muck. But as the wave came, it threw a huge shadow before it and by the time it crested outside the living room window, it blocked out any and all exterior light.

It hit with tremendous force.

The house more than shook; it felt like it had been moved three or four feet. Things were falling from shelves and the plaster was cracking, tiles falling from the ceiling. And then…as the wave pulled back, there was a creaking sound and the picture window collapsed in its frame, a river of mud flowing in, knocking aside a recliner and a coffee table. It winked with shards of glass.

"Back into the dining room!" Marv called.

As they scurried away, taking one of the lanterns with them, he stood in about three or four inches of black, churning muck. Right away, he could see things moving in it. And not one or two worms, but maybe a dozen or more. One of them came up out of the mud and he booted it aside, he fired at another, missed, and hit it with the second round, splitting it nearly in two.

"Watch it!" Tony cried out.

A four-foot worm came out of the sludge, its mud-slicked, heaving body thick and spiny. Its forward segment opened, pulling back and revealing a sheath of needle-sharp teeth, each of which had to be at least an inch or two in length. It moved quickly with a rolling muscular contraction and it would have bit right into his leg if Tony hadn't jumped forward and fired on it. The worms seemed to be made of little more than slime and juice contained in a rubbery envelope of tissue. When the birdshot hit it, it literally exploded into a spray of pulp.

Two others rose up, one making the most obscene sort of croaking noise like a fat bullfrog. Tony fired. But they were everywhere. The mud was a living stew of them and their elastic forms began unwinding from it.

30

"Watch it in there!" Fern heard Marv call to her from the living room and she didn't need to be told twice. She knew damn well what to watch out for. That worm in the drain had been no bizarre evolutionary accident, but one of many. The muck was infested with them.

Kassie was crying and Kalie told her to knock it off. Fern did her best to soothe both of them. They were trembling and so was she. Tony and Marv were shooting and shooting, trying to turn back the tide of the wriggling invaders.

Then...Donna screamed.

She fell back, kicking her leg in the air. One of the worms had gotten into the dining room. Its teeth were buried in her ankle and it was chewing, simply gnawing with a grating sound of knives against bone. Its body undulated with convulsions as it gulped down what it tore loose.

"One side!" Bertie Kalishek said, pushing past Fern and the twins. "One side!"

By then, Donna was nearly out of her mind with pain and hysteria.

Bertie took it all most calmly. She stepped forward, lighting a Lark 100 and pulling two good drags off it as she lowered herself to her knees—no easy process at her age—and took hold of Donna's thrashing leg. When she had it still, she pulled off the cigarette again until the cherry was glowing bright orange...then she stabbed it right into the side of the worm. There was a *ssssttt* sort of sound and the worm reacted immediately, dropping free and writhing on the carpet.

"Don't care for that much, do you, you little vermin?" she said, pulling herself to her feet with aid of the dining room table. When she was up and steady, she stamped down one rain boot on the worm and it burst open in a flood of cold jelly. About six inches of the tail end disengaged itself, squirming wildly about.

"Oh, no you don't," Bertie said and smashed it under her boot. She smashed the head end, too, which was opening and closing its fanged mouth like a fish gasping for air.

Fern called out to Marv that they were okay as she dashed into the bathroom for the first-aid kit.

By then, Donna was looking very pale and very sickly. She was lying flat on the floor, her eyes glazed and barely blinking, her mouth trembling. She was in full view of the twins, of course, who stared down at her with wide eyes. When she made a moaning sound, they cringed and held on to another.

Fern got back and began to dress Donna's ankle. There was a great deal of tissue damage and she'd lost a lot of blood. About all Fern could do under the circumstances was pour some disinfectant on it—which made Donna cry out like she had been scorched with a branding iron—and wrap it up good. She needed real medical care and soon. Fern didn't want to think of the worm's filthy mouth and what sort of germs were already breeding in the wound site.

"Listen," Bertie said. "You hear that?"

They were all hearing it. The worms were massing outside, hissing and making that weird hollow croaking noise. They could hear them sliding along the outer walls of the house and Fern was almost sure there was one up on the roof…a really big one.

"I'm of the opinion we're most definitely in the shit here," Bertie said.

31

Remember when Charise called? You remember when she told you to get out? Well, you should have listened. You should have waded to higher ground or swung tree to tree like a fucking ape, but you should have gotten out.

This was what Tony was thinking as the worms pressed in from every quarter. They were not only coming in through the broken picture window and in such numbers they looked like strings of hamburger being churned out by an old meat grinder, but they were hitting the roof and the other windows like they were being fired from cannons. It made no real sense, but he was seeing it. In the glow of the lantern, they were smashing against the window by the door and with such velocity that they were exploding against the pane until the window was just dark and globby with worm goo.

"Tony!" Marv called out.

Tony avoided a darting worm and almost stepped into the embrace of a much larger one that raised itself from the muck with open jaws. He fired the shotgun and blew the worm into fragments that continued to writhe. He had been momentarily distracted by the sound of other worms punching into the front door, trying to chew their way through.

Together, he and Marv began to back their way toward the dining room.

If this was a battle, then it was one they couldn't hope to win. He was getting low on shells for the shotgun and he figured Marv couldn't have had much more than five or six rounds left for the 30-06.

A huge worm, maybe six or seven feet in length, bashed through one of the few unbroken side panes of the picture window. It was like an immense, swollen tube, segmented and bulging, its mouth suckering open and shut. Tony fired at it, killing it and several smaller ones that clustered around it.

They were going to be buried alive.

There were just too damn many of them.

There was no way in hell they could fight against those kinds of numbers without anything less than a machine gun. And that's when he began to wonder if there wasn't some sort of strategy behind the assault. In a human wave attack, the point was not only to overwhelm defenses and breach perimeters, but to get the defenders to waste the majority of their ammunition.

What if, by some absolute perversion of logic, that's what the worms were doing?

32

It was utter pandemonium, but Fern tried to keep her head.
The twins were holding on to each other so tightly she thought they might break. Donna was in a bad way. Her skin was clammy and damp with sweat. She was unresponsive and trembling. There was no doubt she was in shock or damn close to it. Fern had already raised her damaged leg onto a chair to keep the blood supply limited to the limb and concentrated in her vital organs. That was necessary.

Tony and Marv were still killing worms, but she knew it was a losing battle. Still, there had to be a way. She was not about to let her friends, her husband, and particularly, her *children*, get torn up by those awful things, there was just no damn way.

"Watch it!" Bertie said.

The twins screamed.

A worm came out from under the table and darted at her, burying teeth like darning needles right into the arm of the chair next to her. If it had ideas of freeing itself, Bertie ended that when she chopped it in half with a carving knife from the kitchen. She looked perfectly ridiculous standing there with a cleaver in one hand and a knife in the other, a smoldering Lark 100 hanging from her mouth, her eyes huge and fixed behind her bifocals.

Fern turned and saw Tony and Marv backing their way to the dining room door.

Dear God.

The worms were massing before them. She saw what looked like eight or ten of them that had to be the size of pythons and tangled among them, sliding over them, were what looked like hundreds of smaller worms. They pushed forward like some immense, squirming machine, seeming not to so much crawl as *roll* in a worming, fleshy mass.

"Marv!" she cried out. "Get in here! The both of you get in here!"

Then there was a bolt of pain in her arm. One of them had slipped past Bertie and bitten into her left bicep. Without hesitation, she grabbed its roping, slimy tail and yanked it free, its teeth gnashing madly like the needles of an industrial sewing machine. The only plus was that it had not managed to bite through her denim jacket. She threw it against the wall and it exploded like a wet sack of meat.

They're going to keep coming until they get the twins. What are you going to do about that? Are you going to let these fucking horrors destroy your children or are you going to take action, real action?

There had to be something, something.

And then she remembered the bleach.

33

Marv got Tony behind him and slammed the dining room door shut. It was solid oak. He didn't see how the worms could possibly get through it; then again he couldn't conceive of how any of this had happened in the first place. As he slammed it shut, he severed three worms that were most anxious to join him in the dining room. Another slid over his boot and Tony stomped it.

They were hitting the door now.

At first, it was just a few soft plopping sounds as they struck it almost playfully, but now they were going at it in numbers. *Thump, thump, thump-thump-thump.* The door was holding, but it was trembling in its frame. The worms were not just striking it, they were trying to chew their way through. They were tearing at it and punching into it like whirring drill bits.

Marv had always been a guy who'd prided himself on knowing what to do in a pinch.

But that failed him now.

What *was* there to do?

The worms wanted in and they were going to get in. He thought of Fern and the twins and the horrible way they were going to die and it all weakened him, confused him. He did not know what to do. He couldn't think of a single thing. If they got in, he knew he would fight. He'd use up the last few rounds in his rifle and then he'd go at them with his bare hands. He'd rip dozens to pieces… and then…

That was what he didn't want to think about.

"We need something to drive 'em back with," Tony said at his side. "Fire. We need fire."

Yes, of course. It was one of the oldest of man's defenses against the onslaught of the unknown and nearly always effective.

And that was when Fern screamed.

34

It came from the kitchen.

Another door at the back of the dining room led in there and it was open.

Bertie got there before either Tony or Marv or even the twins. In fact, she charged in there like a barbarian diving into battle. Fern was pressed up against the dishwasher with a jug of Hilex bleach in each hand. An immense worm was bearing down on her. It was a massive, stout thing, inching forward with muscular contractions of its segments, which bulged like inner tubes, flexing and relaxing, flexing and relaxing. The spiny bristles growing from it scraped over the floor with a *scree-scree* sort of sound.

About four feet from Fern, it hesitated.

Maybe it saw it was outnumbered and maybe it sensed its own death in the hating faces of the people gathered there. It looked confused. Its head—or the forward end, at any rate—moved from side to side like it was listening to some unheard melody. Its segments slid back and its mouth opened. For one moment before the teeth unsheathed themselves like the claws of a cat, Fern found herself staring down a pink throat that looked wide enough to swallow her entire leg. Then the worm's orifice made a wet, smacking sound and its gums, soft and mottled, pushed from the mouth and the teeth slid from them like daggers. She saw there was not a single ring of them, but two or three rings, perhaps thirty or more individual teeth glistening like fishhooks.

She knew she didn't have a chance.

Bertie knew she didn't have a chance.

So did Marv and Tony, who didn't dare shoot because from their angle in the doorway, the worm was just too damn close to Fern.

Marv heard the twins whimpering behind him.

He was afraid to move. Afraid he would startle the worm and

it would sink its teeth right into Fern's throat.

But something had to be done and Bertie did it.

As the worm showed its teeth, its head at eye level with Fern, she swore under her breath and threw the cleaver. She hadn't so much as thrown a ball since the 1960s, but she put everything behind it and struck quickly. The worm flinched about a split second before the cleaver sheared right into, slicing neatly through two or three segments. The worm hit the floor, flopping and twisting, its teeth tearing ruts in the kitchen tiles. It pissed a brown ichor from its gaping wound and made a shrill mewling sort of sound as it bunched and contracted, expanding its mass and putting out a river of slime that looked like clear floor wax.

It was Tony who finished it off.

His last two rounds from the Mossberg made an unsightly, liquid mess of the worm. But even rent and splattered and pulverized, shining pieces of it still wriggled in the slime, refusing death.

35

The Hilex bleach worked as good as fire, it turned out. They poured it under both of the doors. The one leading into the living room was the real danger spot. It was weakening, beginning to split in places from the relentless hammering of the very determined worms. Once the bleach was poured under it, there was a flurry of motion from the other side—the sound of soft bodies sliding over one another in a desperate attempt to escape.

Within five minutes, the house was silent.

Completely silent.

The dining room, of course, didn't smell too pretty. The bleach smell reamed out noses and made heads spin, but it was still much better than the alternative.

The survivors waited in the dining room for something else to happen, but nothing did. The only weird thing was that the house trembled once, its timbers creaking as if it was being constricted. In Tony's mind, he thought a very large elephant had just leaned against it. But whatever it was, it never came again.

An hour later, Bertie said, "Must be gone. Quiet out there."

To be on the safe side, they waited another thirty minutes and it was then that they heard what sounded like a helicopter in the distance. It didn't come too close, but close enough to cue everyone in that it was searching for survivors.

"We're going to have to chance it," Marv said.

Tony didn't like the idea, but what he liked even less was the idea of being left behind by a search party and having to spend an entire night waiting for the worms to come.

"Okay," he said. "Let's go."

"Be careful," Fern told them.

"I'll keep an eye on them," Bertie said.

Tony felt a need to be heroic and tell her she was too damned old to be facing danger like this, but from what he'd already seen of her, she was more than capable. Probably a lot more capable than he himself was.

Marv unlocked the door and they all tensed, just waiting for a tidal wave of worms to come flooding into the room. But that didn't happen. He swung the door open and other than the sewer stink and the muck itself, there was nothing.

Nothing at all.

He looked over at Tony and shrugged.

With Bertie trailing behind them, they stepped into the living room. There were no worms anywhere, just a few odd remains. Just to be on the safe side, Marv kept his rifle raised and Tony held a bottle of bleach for quick splashing if it came to that.

"Listen," Bertie said.

Tony expected the very worst, but what he heard was a helicopter. In fact, from his position over near the shattered picture window as he stared out into the muck-drowned neighborhood, he could see a searchlight in the distance scanning above the trees.

"Open that door," Bertie said.

"What?"

"Open it, I said."

She grabbed the lantern as Tony and Marv forced the door open against the muck. She stepped out onto the porch and waved the lantern back and forth. "OVER HERE!" she shouted. "OVER HERE, GODDAMMIT!"

She was making a good effort of it, that was for sure.

Marv was at the picture window and Tony was right behind her. The night was dim, the moon hidden in a pocket of dark clouds. Things were quiet out there, save for the sound of the chopper's rotors. Bertie waved her lantern back and forth. But as to whether she was seen was anybody's guess. The helicopter banked to the right and disappeared.

"Ah...you useless sonsofabitches," she said.

Tony heard a splashing like waves breaking on a beach and a stink wafted in through the door like that of a cesspool at high summer...moist and green and almost fruiting with filth.

"Get back inside! Get back inside!" Marv cried in a frantic voice. "*Bertie, get the fuck back inside!*"

Tony looked out past Bertie into the night which was backlit somewhat by the streetlamp across the street. He saw a shape. An unbelievably huge shape moving out of the darkness with a juicy, rubbery sort of sound like a wet intestine pulled from a belly. For one insane moment, he was not really sure what he was looking at...it was like the darkness was splitting open to reveal a glistening black tunnel...but then he saw and he knew: it was the immense maw of an absolutely colossal worm.

That was why Marv cried out, why he was making a mad dash toward the door where Tony stood in moonstruck terror.

The mouth yawned open and a set of spongy pink shining gums jutted forth, mammoth teeth sliding from them like switchblades. It took but a fraction of a second for Tony to see this and for it to register in his mind. By the time Marv got within feet of him, the monster worm had taken Bertie, who had about enough time to say, "Oh, shit," and then blood exploded in Tony's face like a summer squall, blinding him and making him cry out.

It happened so fast he thought the worm had just struck at her like an adder, but that's not what happened at all. By the time she realized the worm was even there, it was maybe ten feet from her. Its mouth opened and for one insane moment it looked like it had vomited out a dozen yellow, gleaming cobras. They were in fact tongues that moved with a squirming peristalsis, their razored tips spearing into her like hypodermic needles, impaling her completely and this was what made the blood spray out of her like a hydrant had been opened.

About the time Tony hit the floor, the tongues yanked Bertie into the worm's jaws and the teeth came down, splitting her open like a piñata, her bones cracking like walnuts. Her upper torso dangled from its mouth and the incredible pressure of the jaws made her dentures fly from her mouth along with a mist of blood. Her eyes popped from their sockets and her guts were forced up her throat. Then it sucked her all the way in and she was gnawed and chewed before being drawn down the canalicular tunnel of its throat.

As Marv got to the door, Bertie was pulled up and away.

The moon came out from behind a cloud and showed him the thing in all its hideous grandeur. Rising up thirty feet from the muck, it was a cyclopean and shivering thing like a row of train cars standing on end, a monstrous tower of pale, pink, pulsating flesh composed of multiple ringlike segments, each of which were inflated as big around as the opening of a train tunnel...in fact, as he watched, they expanded until they were even much *larger*, secreting a sea of foaming slime that spread out over the muck.

It rose up against the full moon, its mouth yawning ever wider into a vast dark hole shining with rows upon rows of spikelike teeth, dripping copious amounts of black bile in six-foot elastic ribbons that swung back and forth with its awful boneless, corkscrewing motion.

Tony didn't see as much of it as Marv did—he was busy pawing Bertie's blood from his face—but he saw enough to know they were in serious trouble because it was easily big enough to flatten a two-story house with its surging, gelatinous bulk. Maybe it had risen up thirty feet and perhaps more, wavering from side to side over the rooftops and trees, but there was a lot more of it still in the muck and probably more yet in whatever fusty crawl space it had slithered up from.

Marv had his rifle in his hands, but he felt entirely impotent.

He didn't think even a .50-caliber machine gun would do much damage to the thing. But the rifle was all he had.

It was then that he noticed the worm was not just some giant B-movie-sized vermin, but the Mother Worm: the source, the epicenter, the fucking black pupating womb of them all. Its underside, from where it rose from the rippling muck to maybe a dozen segments from the mouth, was a convulsive nursery of worms. Hundreds of them hung from it like the remoras on a shark's belly, coiling fleshy tubes, some only a few feet in length and others six or seven feet. The large ones were dropping free and as they did so, smaller ones pushed forth from the jellied flesh of the Mother Worm. She was a great biological machine, a squirming incubator that could have drowned the world in her larvae given time.

She let go with a mewling, echoing cry that got louder and louder until it shrilled like an air-raid siren as if she were calling out her victory over the world of men.

As the house shook and everyone covered their ears and Fern cried out, wanting to know what was going on, Marv, from his position in the doorway, worked the bolt on his 30-06 and fired up at the thing, the bullet drilling into it and through it. The worm barely trembled.

"FUCK ARE YOU DOING?" Tony shouted at him.

But Marv wasn't really sure himself, but in the back of his mind an insane, last-ditch sort of defense had occurred to him and if things had not been so tense, so surreal, so deadly with grim possibility, he would never have considered it...but desperation was the mother of invention.

The Mother Worm must have felt the round drill through her, minimal as it was in comparison to her nightmare vastness. She rippled and writhed with undulant gyrations, curling like an inchworm and striking at the house. She took out what remained of the picture window and the frame that held it. The walls cracked. Plaster fell. Bricks were pulverized to powder. The impact actually shifted the house a few feet on its foundation.

She hit the house again, striking the door this time and widening it to the girth of a garage door. One more strike and she would be in.

As she hit the door, Tony scrambled away on his hands and knees, her jutting yellow tongues stabbing out at him, brushing over the soles of his boots and slitting the sofa open.

Marv did not retreat.

It was all or nothing now.

As the Mother Worm brought her head up high above the house to cry out again, he got in position with his rifle at the missing picture window. He had a clear shot if he could just make it happen, if he could just put one round where it needed to go.

On his knees, the stock against his shoulder, he tightened the field on the scope and fired at the power line that was strung between two utility poles and dangling above the rising coils of the worm in the mud. He fired and missed. *Shit*. He fired again and this time he knew he was close because he split the telecom line which dropped away harmlessly.

Breathing slow and deep, knowing the worm was about to make her last and most devastating strike, the muck around her seeping with the forms of her children, he sighted in on the power line. For a professional shooter or sniper, it would have been an easy shot...for a guy who popped a deer every few years and maybe hit the range a few weeks a year, it was tricky.

He remained calm.

He steadied his nerves.

The line was directly in his sights. Exhaling air between clenched teeth, he squeezed off a round...and it hit. The power line was easily split, throwing a shower of blue sparks and dropping directly onto the Mother Worm where it grounded itself out.

The effect was instantaneous.

The Mother Worm writhed and twisted and coiled. She snapped back and forth like a bullwhip, shattering houses across the street, turning garages into kindling and flattening cars like beer cans. And the more she struggled, the more she ensnared herself in the power line, which fed over 13,000 volts directly into her hide. The muck around her was bubbling and steaming, her young popping like ticks from the heat. She boiled from the inside out, throwing out plumes of churning steam. As she whipped and looped with spasms, huge rents split open her segments and spewed burning tissue and blazing slime until she burst into flame, rising up one last time like a blackened Fourth of July snake before crashing into the muck and breaking apart.

Then there was silence.

Silence for five or ten seconds.

Then Tony said, "I think I fucking pissed myself."

Marv stumbled into the dining room where his wife and children were waiting for him. He pulled them close to him in a huge bear hug. He could hear the choppers coming. The remains of the Mother Worm were still smoldering and burning in the street. A few houses had lit up with her, flickering like candles.

"Are...are they gone?" Kassie asked. "Are the worms gone?"

"Yes," Marv told her. "They're gone."

And though it was still dark out, night had ended on Pine Street.

About the Author

Tim Curran is the author of the novels Skin Medicine, Hive, Dead Sea, Resurrection, Hag Night, Skull Moon, The Devil Next Door, Doll Face, Afterburn, House of Skin, and Biohazard. His short stories have been collected in Bone Marrow Stew and Zombie Pulp. His novellas include The Underdwelling, The Corpse King, Puppet Graveyard, Worm, and Blackout. His short stories have appeared in such magazines as City Slab, Flesh&Blood, Book of Dark Wisdom, and Inhuman, as well as anthologies such as Shadows Over Main Street, Eulogies III, and October Dreams II. His fiction has been translated into German, Japanese, Spanish, and Italian. Find him on Facebook at: https://www.facebook.com/tim.curran.77

Bibliography

Novels

Afterburn
Biohazard
Cannibal Corpse
Dead Sea
Doll Face
Graveworm
Grim Riders
Grimweave
Hag Night
Hive
Hive 2: The Spawning
House of Skin
Long Black Coffin
Monstrosity
Nightcrawlers
Resurrection
Skin Medicine
Skull Moon
Terror Cell
The Devil Next Door

Novellas

Blackout
Corpse Rider
Deadlock
Fear Me
Headhunter
Leviathan
Puppet Graveyard
Sow
Tenebris
The Corpse King
The Underdwelling
Toxic Shadows
Worm

Collections

Bone Marrow Stew
Here There be Monsters
Zombie Pulp

Curious about other Crossroad Press books?
Stop by our site:
https://www.crossroadpress.com
We offer quality writing
in digital, audio, and print formats.